THIS BOOK BELONGS TO: -

Robinson Crusoe

Robinson Crusoe

Daniel Defoe

Cover illustration by
Deno Caruana

Published by Priory Books, Bridlington.
A Peter Haddock Limited imprint.
© B. W. (Leicester) Limited.

CHAPTER ONE

I was born in the year 1632, in the city of York, of a good family. I had two elder brothers, one of whom was lieutenant-colonel of an English regiment of foot in Flanders, and was killed at the battle near Dunkirk against the Spaniards; what became of my second brother I never knew, any more than my father or mother did know what was become of me.

One day at Hull, where I went casually, one of my companions being going to sea to London in his father's ship and prompting me to go with them with the common allurement of seafaring men — namely, that it should cost me nothing for my passage. Never any young adventurer's misfortunes, I believe, began sooner, or continued longer than mine. The ship was no sooner gotten out of the Humber but the wind began to blow, and the waves to rise in a most frightful manner; and, as I had never been to sea before, I was most inexpressibly sick in body, and terrified in my mind.

By this time it blew a terrible storm indeed, and now I began to see terror and amazement in the faces even of the seamen themselves.

The storm was so violent, that I saw what is not often seen — the master, the boatswain, and some others more sensible than the rest, at their prayers, and expecting every moment when the ship would go to the bottom. In the middle of the night, and under all the rest of our distresses, one of the men that had been down on purpose to see, cried out we had sprung a leak; another said there was four foot of water in the hold.

Then all hands were called to the pump. At that very word my heart, as I thought, died within me, and I fell backwards upon the side of my bed where I sat, into the cabin. Howewer, the men roused me, and told me that I that was able to do nothing before was as well able to pump as another, at which I stirred up and went to the pump.

We worked on; but the water increasing in the hold, it was apparent that the ship would founder; and though the storm began to abate a little, yet, as it was not possible she could swim till we might run into a port, so the master continued firing guns for help, and a light ship, who had ridden it out just ahead of us, ventured a boat out to help us. It was with the utmost hazard the boat came near us; but it was impossible for us to get on board, or for the boat to lie near the ship's side, till at last, the men rowing very heartily, and venturing their lives to save ours, our men cast them a rope over the stern with a buoy to it, and then veered it out a great length, which they, after great labour and hazard, took hold of, and we hauled them close under our stern, and got all into their boat. It was of no purpose for them or us after we were in the boat to think of reaching their own ship, so all agreed to let her drive, and only to pull her in towards shore as much as we could; and our master promised them, that if the boat was staved upon shore, he would make it good to their master; so, partly rowing and partly driving, our boat went away to the norward, sloping towards the shore almost as far as Winterton Ness.

We were not much more than a quarter of an hour out of our ship when we saw her sink, and then I understood for the first time what was meant by a ship foundering in the sea.

While we were in this condition, the men yet labouring at the oar to bring the boat near the shore, we could see, when our boat, mounting the waves, a great many people running along the shore to assist us when we should come near; but we made but slow way, nor were we able to reach the shore, till, being past the lighthouse at Winterton, the shore falls off to the westward towards Cromer, and so the land broke off a little the violence of the wind. Here we got in, and though not without much difficulty, got all safe on shore, and walked afterwards on foot to Yarmouth, where, as unfortunate men, we were used with great humanity, as well by the magistrates of the town, who assigned us good quarters, as by particular merchants and owners of ships, and had money given us sufficient to carry us either to London or back to Hull, as we thought fit.

Had I now had the sense to have gone back to Hull, and have gone home, I had been happy. But my ill fate pushed me on now with an obstinacy that nothing could resist.

My comrade, who had helped to harden me before, and who was the master's son, was now less forward than I. The first time he spoke to me after we were at Yarmouth, it appeared his tone was altered, and looking very melancholy, and shaking his head, asked me how I did, and telling his father who I was, and how I had come this voyage only for a trial, in order to go farther abroad. His father, turning to me with a very grave and concerned tone, "Young man," says he, "you ought never to go to sea any more; you ought to take this for a plain and visible token that you are not to be a seafaring man."

We parted soon after, for I made him little answer, and I saw him no more. Which way he went I know not. As for me, having some money in my pocket, I travelled to London by land; and there, as well as on the road, had many struggles with myself — what course of life I should take, and wheather I should go home or go to sea.

As to going home, shame opposed the best motions that offered to my thoughts: and it immediately occurred to me how I should be laughed at among the neighbours, and should be ashamed to see, not my father and mother only, but even everybody else.

It was my lot first of all to fall into pretty good company in London, which does not always happen to such loose and unguided young fellows as I then was, the devil generally not omitting to lay some snare for them very early. But it was not so with me. I first fell acquainted with the master of a ship who had been on the coast of Guinea; and who, having had very good success there, was resolved to go again; and who, taking a fancy to my conversation, which was not at all disagreeable at that time, hearing me say I had a mind to see the world, told me if I would go to the voyage with him I should be at no expense; I should be his messmate and his companion; and if I could carry anything with me, I should have all the advantage of it that the trade would admit, and perhaps I might meet with some encouragement.

I embraced the offer, and, entering into a strict friendship with this captain, who was an honest and plain-dealing man, I went the voyage with him, and carried a small adventure with me, which, by the disinterested honesty of my friend the captain, I increased very considerably; for I carried about £40 in such toys and trifles as the captain directed me to buy. This £40 I had mustered together by the assistance of some of my relations whom I corresponded with, and who, I believe, got my father, or at least my mother, to contribute so much as that to my first adventure.

This was the only voyage which I may say was successful in all my adventures, and which I owe to the integrity and honesty of my friend the captain, under whom also I got a competent knowledge of the mathematics and the rules of navigation, learned how to keep an account of the ship's course, take an observation, and, in short, to understand some things that were needful to be understood by a sailor. For, as he took delight to introduce me, I took delight to learn; and, in a word, this voyage made me both a sailor and a merchant; for I brought home five pounds nine ounces of gold dust for my adventure, which yielded me in London at my return almost £300, and this filled me with those aspiring thoughts which have since so completed my ruin.

I was now set up for a Guinea trader: and my friend, to my great misfortune, dying soon after his arrival, I resolved to go the same voyage again, and I embarked in the same vessel with one who was his mate in the former voyage, and had now got the command of the ship. This was the unhappiest voyage that ever man made; for though I did not carry quite £100 of my new gained wealth, so that I had £200 left, and which I lodged with my friend's widow, who was very just to me, yet I fell into terrible misfortunes in this voyage; and the first was this — namely, our ship making her course towards the Canary Islands, or rather between those islands and the African shore, was surprised in the grey of the morning by a Turkish rover of Sallee, who gave chase to us with all the sail she could make.

He prepared to attack us, and we to defend ourselves; but laying us on board, he entered sixty men upon our decks, who immediately fell to cutting and hacking the decks and rigging. We plied them with small-shot, half-pikes, powder-chests, and such like, and cleared our deck of them twice. However, to cut short this melancholy part of our story, our ship being disabled, and three of our men killed and eight wounded, we were obliged to yield, and were carried all prisoners into Sallee, a port belonging to the Moors.

The usage I had there was not so dreadful as at first I apprehended, nor was I carried up the country to the emperor's court, as the rest of our men were, but was kept by the captain of the rover as his proper prize, and made his slave, being young and nimble and fit for his business.

As my new patron or master had taken me home to his house, so I was in hopes that he would take me with him when he went to sea again, believing that it would some time or other be his fate to be taken by a Spanish or Portugal man-of-war; and that then I should be set at liberty. But this hope of mine was soon taken away; for when he went to sea he left me on shore to look after his little garden, and do the common drudgery of slaves about his house; and then when he came home again from his cruise, he ordered me to lie in the cabin to look after the ship.

Here I meditated nothing but my escape, and what method I might take to effect it, but found no way that had the least probability in it. Nothing presented to make the supposition of it rational; for I had nobody to communicate it to that would embark with me, no fellow-slave, no Englishman, Irishman, or Scotsman there but myself; so that for two years, though I often pleased myself with the imagination, yet I never had the least encouraging prospect of putting it in practice.

After about two years an odd circumstance presented itself, which put the old thought of making some attempt for my liberty again in my head. My patron lying at home longer than usual without fitting out his ship, which, as I heard, was for want of money, he used constantly, once or twice a week, sometimes oftener, if the weather was fair, to take the ship's pinnace, and go out into the road a-fishing; and as he always took me and a young Maresco with him to row the boat, we made him very merry, and I proved very dexterous in catching fish, insomuch that sometimes he would send me with a

Moor, one of his kinsmen, and the youth — the Maresco, as they called him — to catch a dish of fish for him.

It happened one time, that going a-fishing in a calm morning, a fog rose so thick, that though we were not half a league from the shore we lost sight of it; rowing we knew not whither or which way, we laboured all day and all the next night, and when the morning came we found we had pulled off to sea instead of pulling in for the shore; and that we were at least two leagues from the shore. Howewer, we got well in again, though with a great deal of labour and some danger; for the wind began to blow pretty fresh in the morning, but particulary we were all very hungry.

But our patron, warned by this disaster, resolved to take more care of himself for the future; and having lying by him the long-boat of our English ship he had taken, he resolved he would not go a-fishing any more without a compass and some provision. So he ordered the carpenter of his ship, who also was an English slave, to build a little state-room or cabin in the middle of the long-boat, like that of a barge, with a place to stand behind it to steer and hale home the main-sheet; and room before for a hand or two to stand and work the sails. She sailed with what we call a shoulder-of-mutton sail; and the boom jibbed over the top of the cabin, which lay very snug and low, and had in it room for him to lie, with a slave or two; and a table to eat on, with some small lockers to put in some bottles of such liquor as he thought fit to drink: particulary his bread, rice, and coffee.

We went frequently out with his boat a-fishing. And as I was most dexterous to catch fish for him, he never went without me. It happened that he had appointed to go out in this boat, either for pleasure or fishing, with two or three Moors of some distinction in that place and for whom he had provided extraordinarily, and had therefore sent on board the boat overnight a larger store of provisions than ordinary; and had ordered me to get ready three fuses with powder and shot, which were on board his ship, for that they designed some sport of fowling as well as fishing.

I got all things ready as he had directed, and waited the next morning with the boat washed clean, and everything to accommodate his guests. When by and by my patron came on board alone, and told me his guests had put off going, upon some business that fell out, and ordered me with the man and boy as usual to go out with the boat and catch them some fish, for that his friends were to sup at his house; and commanded that as soon as I had got some fish, I should bring it home to his house; all which I prepared to do.

This moment my former notions of deliverance darted into my thought, for now I found I was like to have a little ship at my command; and my master being gone, I prepared to furnish myself, not for a fishing business, but for a voyage; though I knew not, neither did I so much as consider, whither I should steer; for anywhere to get out of that place was my way.

My first contrivance was to make a pretence to speak to this Moor, to get something for our subsistence on board; for I told him we must not presume to eat of our patron's bread. He said that was true;

so he brought a large basket of rusk or biscuit of their kind, and three jars with fresh water into the boat. I knew where my patron's case of bottles stood, which it was evident by the make were taken out of some English prize, and I conveyed them into the boat while the Moor was on shore, as if they had been there before for our master. I conveyed also a great lump of beeswax into the boat, which weighed above half a hundred-weight, with a parcel of twine and thread, a hatchet, a saw, and a hammer, all which were of great use to us afterwards specially the wax to make candles.

Thus furnished with everything needful, we sailed out of the port to fish. The wind blew from the north-north-east, which was contrary to my desire; for had it blown southerly, I had been sure to have made the coast of Spain, and at least reached to the Bay of Cadiz; but my resolutions were, blow which way it would, I would be gone from that horrid place where I was, and leave the rest to fate.

As I had the helm, I run the boat out near a league farther, and then brought her to, as if I would fish; when giving the boy the helm, I stepped forward to where the Moor was, and making as if stooping for something behind him, I took him by surprise with my arm under his legs, and tossed him clear overboard into the sea. He rose immediately, for he swam like a cork, and called to me, begged to be taken in; told me he would go all over the world with me. He swam so strong after the boat that he would have reached me very quickly, there being but little wind; upon which I stepped into the cabin, and fetching one of the fowling pieces, I presented it at him, and told him I had done him no hurt, and if he would be quiet I would do him none. So he turned himself about and swam for the shore; and I make no doubt but he reached it with ease, for he was an excellent swimmer.

When he was gone I turned to the boy, who they called Xury, and said to him, "Xury, if you will be faithful to me, I'll make you a great man; but if you will not stroke your face to be true to me — that is, swear by Mahomet and his father's beard — I must throw you into the sea too." The boy smiled in my face, and spoke so innocently, that I could not mistrust him; and swore to be faithful to me and go all over the world with me.

As soon as it grew dark in the evening I changed my course, and steered directly south and by east, bending by course a little toward the east, that I might keep in with the shore; and having a fair fresh gale of wind and a smooth, quiet sea, I made such sail that I believe by the next day at three o'clock in the afternoon, when I first made the land, I could not be less than 150 miles south of Sallee; quite beyond the Emperor of Morocco's dominions, or, indeed, of any other kind thereabouts, for we saw no people.

So I ventured to make the coast, and came to an anchor in the mouth of a little river, I knew not what, or where; neither what latitude, what country, what nation, or what river. I neither saw, nor desired to see, any people; the principal thing I wanted was fresh water. We came into this creek in the evening, resolved to swim on shore as soon as it was dark, and discover the country; but as soon as it was quite dark we heard such dreadful noises of the barking, rearing, and howling of wild creatures, of we knew not what kinds, that the poor boy was ready to die with fear, and begged of me not to go on shore.

But we found afterwards that we need not take such pains for water, for a little higher up the creek where we were, we found the water fresh when the tide was out, which flowed but a little way up.

After this stop we made on to the southward continually for ten or twelve days, living very sparing on our provisions, which began to abate very much, and going no oftener into the shore than we were obliged to for fresh water. My design in this was to make the river Gambia or Senegal — that is to say, anywhere about the Cape de Verde, where I was in hopes to meet with some European ship.

When I had pursued this resolution about ten days longer, as I have said, I began to see that the land was inhabited; and in two or three places, as we sailed by, we saw people stand upon the shore to look at us. We could also perceive they were quite black. I was once inclined to have gone on shore to have speech with them. But Xury was my better counsellor, and said to me, "No go, no go." However, I hauled in nearer the shore that I might talk to them, and I found they ran along the shore by me a good way.

I observed they had no weapons in their hands — except one, who had a long slender stick, which Xury said was a lance, and that they would throw them a great way with good aim. So I kept at a distance, but talked with them by signs as well as I could; and particulary made signs for something to eat. They beckoned to me to stop my boat, and they would fetch me some meat. Upon this, I lowered the top of my sail and lay by; and two of them ran up into the country, and in less than half an hour came back and brought with them two pieces of dry flesh and some corn, such as is the produce of their country — but we neither knew what the one or the other was. However, we were willing to accept it, but how to come at it was our next dispute; for I was not for venturing on shore to them, and they were as much afraid of us. But they took a safe way for us all — for they brought it to the shore and laid it down, and went and stood a great way off till we fetched it on board, and then came close to us again.

Then I made signs to them for some water, and held out one of my jars to them, turning it bottom upward, to show that it was empty, and that I wanted to have it filled. They called immediately to some of their friends; and there came two women, and brought a great vessel made of earth, and burned as I suppose in the sun. This they set down for me as before; and I sent Xury on shore with my jars, and filled them all three.

I was now furnished with roots and corn — such as it was — and water; and leaving my friendly negroes, I made forward for about eleven days more without offering to go near the shore, till I saw the land run out a great length into the sea, at about the distance of four or five leagues before me, and the sea being very calm, I kept a large offing to make this point. At length doubling the point at about two leagues from the land, I saw plainly land on the other side to seaward. Then I concluded, as I was most certain indeed, that this was the Cape de Verde Islands. However, they were at a great distance; and I could not well tell what I had best do, for if I should be taken with a fresh of wind, I might neither reach one nor the other.

In this dilemma, as I was very pensive, I stepped into the cabin and sat me down, Xury having the helm, when on a sudden the boy cried out, "Master, master, a ship with a sail!" and the foolish boy was frightened out of his wits, thinking it must needs be some of his master's ships sent to pursue us, when I knew we were gotten far enough out of their reach. I jumped out of the cabin, and immediately saw not only the ship, but what she was — namely, that it was a Portuguese ship, and, as I thought, was bound to the coast of Guinea for negroes. But when I observed the course she steered I was soon convinced they were bound some other way, and did not design to come any nearer to the shore. Upon which I stretched out to sea as much as I could, resolving to speak with them if possible.

With all the sail I could make, I found I should not be able to come in their way, but that they would be gone by before I could make any signal to them. But after I had crowded to the utmost and began to despair, they, it seems, saw me by the help of their perspective-glasses, and that it was some European boat, which, as they supposed, must belong to some ship that was lost; so they shortened sail to let me come up: I was encouraged with this; and as I had my patron's ancient on board, I made a waft of it to which they saw, for they told me that they saw the smoke, though they did not hear the gun. Upon these signals they very kindly brought to, and lay by for me, and in about three hours' time I came up with them.

CHAPTER TWO

They asked me what I was, in Portuguese and in Spanish and in French, but I understood none of them; but at last a Scottish sailor who was on board called to me; and I answered him, and told him I was an Englishman, that I had made my escape out of slavery from the Moors at Sallee. Then they bade me come on board, and very kindly took me in and all my goods.

It was an inexpressible joy to me — that any one will believe — that I was thus delivered, as I esteemed it, from such a miserable and almost hopeless condition as I was in, and I immediately offered all I had to the captain of the ship as a return for my deliverance; but he generously told me he would take nothing from me, but that all I had should be delivered safe to me when I came to the Brazils.

As he was charitable in his proposal, so he was just in the performance to a tittle; for he ordered the seamen that none should offer to touch anything I had. Then he took everything into his own possession, and gave me back an exact inventory of them, that I might have them, even so much as my three earthen jars.

As to my boat it was a very good one, and that he saw, and told me he would buy it of me for the ship's use, and asked me what I would have for it? I told him he had been so generous to me in everything, that I could not offer to make any price of the boat, but left it entirely to him; upon which he told me he would give me a note of his hand to pay me eighty pieces of eight for it at Brazil, and when it came there, if anyone offered to give more, he would make it up. He offered me also sixty pieces of eight for my boy Xury; which I was loath to take: not that I was not willing to let the captain have him, but I was very loath to sell the poor boy's liberty, who had assisted me so faithfully in procuring my own. However, when I let him know my reason, he owned it to be just, and offered me this medium — that he would give the boy an obligation to set him free in ten years, if he turned Christian. Upon this, and Xury saying he was willing to go to him, I let the captain have him.

We had a very good voyage to the Brazils, and arrived in the Bay de Todos los Santos, or All-Saints' Bay, in about twenty-two days after. And now I was once more delivered from the most miserable of all conditions of life; and what to do next with myself I was now to consider.

The generous treatment the captain gave me I can never enough remember. He would take nothing of me for my passage, and caused everything I had in the ship to be punctually delivered me; and what I was willing to sell he bought, such as the case of bottles, two of my guns, and a piece of the rest. In a word, I made about two hundred and twenty pieces of eight of all my cargo; and with this stock I went on shore in the Brazils.

I had not been long here, but being recommended to the house of a good honest man like himself, who had an ingeino, as they call it — that is, a plantation and a sugar-house — I lived with him some time, and acquainted myself by that means with the manner of their planting and making of sugar. And seeing how well the planters lived, and how they grew rich suddenly, I resolved, if I could get license to settle there, I would turn planter among them; resolving in the meantime to find out some way to get my money which I had left in London remitted to me.

Had I continued in the station I was now in, I had room for all the happy things to have yet befallen me for which my father so earnestly recommended a quiet, retired life.

As I had once done thus in my breaking away from my parents, so I could not be content now, but I must go and leave the happy view I had of being a rich and thriving man in my new plantation, only to pursue a rash and immoderate desire of rising faster than the nature of the thing admitted.

You may suppose that having now lived almost four years in the Brazils, and beginning to thrive and prosper very well upon my plantation, I had not only learned the language, but had contracted acquintance and friendship among my fellow-planters, as well as among the merchants of St. Salvadore, which was our port; and that, in my discourses among them, I had frequently given them an account of my two voyages to the coast of Guinea, the manner of trading with the negroes there, and how easy it was to purchase upon the coast for trifles — such as beads, toys, knives, scissors, hatchets, bits of glass, and the like — not only gold dust, Guinea grains, elephant's teeth, &c., but negroes for the service of the Brazils in great numbers.

They listened always very attentively to my discourses on these heads, but especially to that part which related to the buying negroes; which was a trade at that time not only not far entered into, but, as far as it was, had been carried on by the **assiento,** or permission of the Kings of Spain and Portugal, and engrossed in the public; so that few negroes were brought, and those excessively dear.

It happened, being in company with some merchants and planters of my acquaintance, and talking of those things very earnestly, three of them came to me the next morning. And after enjoining me to secrecy, they told me that they had a mind to fit out a ship to go to Guinea; that they had all plantations as well as I, and were straitened for nothing so much as servants; that as it was a trade that could not be carried on, because they could not publicly sell the negroes when they came home, so they desired to make but one voyage, to bring the negroes on shore privately, and divide them among their own or I would go as their supercargo in the ship to manage the trading part upon the coast of Guinea. And they offered me that I should have my equal share of the negroes, without providing any part of the stock.

This was a fair proposal, it must be confessed, had it been made to any one that not had a settlement and plantation of his own to look after, which was in a fair way of coming to be very considerable, and with a good stock upon it. But for me that was thus entered and established, and had nothing to do but go on as I had begun for three or four years more, and who in that time, and with that little addition, could scarce have failed of being worth three or four thousand pounds sterling, and that increasing too — for me to think of such a voyage was the most preposterous thing that ever man in such circumstances could be guilty of.

I told them I would go with all my heart if they would undertake to look after my plantation in my absence, and would dispose of it to such as I should direct if I miscarried. This they all engaged to do, and entered into writings or convenants to do so; and I made a formal will, disposing of my plantation and effects, in case of my death, making the captain of the ship that had saved my life, as before, my universal heir, but obliging him to dispose of my effects as I had directed in my will — one-half of the produce being to himself, and the other to be shipped to England.

Our ship was about 120 ton burthen; carried six guns and fourteen men, besides the master, his boy, and myself. We had on board no large cargo of goods, except of such toys as were fit for our trade with the negroes — such as beads, bits of glass, shells and odd trifles, especially little looking-glasses, knives, scissors, hatchets, and the like.

The same day I went on board we set sail, standing away to the northwards upon our own coast, with design to stretch over for the African coast when they came about 10 or 12 degrees of northern latitude; which, it seems, was the manner of their course in those days. We had very good weather, only excessively hot, all the way upon our own coast, till we came to the height of Cape St. Augustino; from whence, keeping farther off at sea, we lost sight of land, and steered as if we were bound for the Isle Fernand de Noronha, holding our course north-east by north, and leaving those isles on the east. In this course we passed the line in about twelve days' time; and were by our last observation in 7 degrees 22 minutes northern latitude, when a violent tornado or hurricane took us quite out of our knowledge. It began from the south-east; from whence it blew in such a terrible manner that for twelve days together we could do nothing but drive, and, scudding away before it, let it carry us whither even fate and the fury of the winds directed. And during these twelve days I need not say that I expected every day to be swallowed up; nor, indeed, did any in the ship expect to save their lives.

In this distress, we had, besides the terror of the storm, one of our men died of the calenture, and one man and the boy washed overboard. About the twelfth day, the weather abating a little, the master made an observation as well as he could, and found that he was in about 11 degrees north latitude, but that he was 22 degrees of longitude difference west from Cape St. Augustino; so that he found he was gotten upon the coast of Guinea, or the north part of Brazil, beyond the river Amazones, toward that of the river Oronoque, commonly called the Great River, and began to consult with me what course should take, for the ship was leaky and very much disabled, and he was going directly back to the coast of Brazil.

I was positively against that; and looking over the charts of the sea-coast of America with him, we concluded that there was no inhabited country for us to have recourse to till we came within the circle of the Carribbe Islands, and therefore resolved to stand away for Barbadoes; which, by keeping off at sea, to avoid the indraught of the Bay or Gulf of Mexico, we might easily perform, as we hoped, in about fifteen days' sail; whereas we could not possibly make our voyage to the coast of Africa without some assistance both to our ship and to ourselves.

With this design we changed our course, and steered away north-west by west, in order to reach some of our English Islands, where I hoped for relief. But our voyage was otherwise determined; for, being in the latitude of 12 degrees 18 minutes, a second storm came upon us, which carried us away with the same impetuosity westward, and drove us so out of the very way of all human commerce, that had all our lives been saved as to the sea, we were rather in danger of being devoured by savages than ever returning to our own country.

In this distress, the wind still blowing very hard, one of our men early in the morning cried out "Land!" and we had no sooner run out of the cabin to look out in hopes of seeing whereabouts in the world we were, but the ship struck upon a sand, and in a moment, her motion being so stopped, the sea broke over her in such a manner, that we expected we should all have perished immediately, and we were immediately driven into our close quarters to shelter us from the very foam and spray of the sea.

It is not easy for anyone who has not been in the like condition to describe or conceive the consternation of men in such circumstances. We knew nothing where we were, or upon what land it was we were driven, whether an island or the main, whether inhabited or not inhabited; and as the rage of the wind was still great, though rather less than at first, we could not so much as hope to have the ship hold many minutes without breaking in pieces, unless the winds by a kind of miracle should turn immediately about.

Now, though the wind did a little abate, yet the ship having thus struck upon the sand, and sticking too fast for us to expect her getting off, we were in a dreadful condition indeed, and had nothing to do but to think of saving our lives as well as we could. We had a boat at our stern just before the storm, but she was first staved by dashing against the ship's rudder, and in the next place she broke away, and either sunk or was driven off to sea; so there was no hope from her. We had another boat on board; but how to get her off into the sea was a doubtful thing. However, there was no room to debate, for we fancied the ship would break in pieces every minute, and some told us she was actually broken already.

In this distress the mate of our vessel lays hold of the boat, and with the help of the rest of the men they got her slung over the ship's side, and getting all into her, let go, and committed ourselves, being eleven in number, to God's mercy and the wild sea; for though the storm was abated considerably, yet the sea went dreadfully high upon the shore.

And now our case was very dismal indeed; for we all saw plainly that the sea went so high that the boat could not live, and that we should be inevitably drowned. As to making sail, we had none; nor if we had, could we have done anything with it; so we worked at the oar towards the land, though with heavy hearts, like men going to execution; for we all knew that when the boat came nearer the shore she would be dashed in a thousand pieces by the breach of the sea. However, we committed our souls to God in the most earnest manner, and the wind driving us towards the shore we hastened our destruction with our own hands, pulling as well as we could towards land.

What the shore was — whether rock or sand, whether steep or shoal — we knew not; the only hope that could rationally give us the least shadow of expectation was, if we might happen into some bay or gulf, or the mouth of some river, where by great chance we might have run our boat in, or got under the lee of the land, and perhaps made smooth water. But there was nothing of this appeared; but as we made nearer and nearer the shore, the land looked more frightful than the sea.

After we had rowed or rather driven about a league and a half, as we reckoned it, a raging wave, mountain-like, came rolling astern of us, and plainly bade us expect the **coup de grâce**. In a word, it took us with such a fury, that it overset the boat at once, and separating us as well from the boat as from one another, gave us not time hardly to say, O God! for we were all swallowed up in a moment.

Nothing can describe the confusion of thought which I felt when I sunk into the water; for though I swam very well, yet I could not deliver myself from the waves so as to draw breath, till that a wave, having driven me or rather carried me a vast way on towards the shore, and having spent itself, went back, and left me upon the land almost dry, but half-dead with the water I took in. I had so much presence of mind as well as breath left that, seeing myself nearer the mainland than I expected, I got upon my feet, and endeavoured to make on towards the land as fast as I could before another wave should return and take me up again. My business was to hold my breath and rise myself upon the water if I could, and so by swimming to preserve my breathing and pilot myself towards the shore if possible; my greatest concern now being that the sea, as it would carry me a great way towards the shore when it came on, might not carry me back again with it.

The wave that came upon me again buried me at once twenty or thirty feet deep in its own body; and I could feel myself carried with a mighty force and swiftness towards the shore a very great way; but I held my breath, and assisted myself to swim still forward with all my might. I was ready to burst with holding my breath, when, as I felt myself rising up, so to my immediate relief I found my head and hands shoot out above the surface of the water; and though it was not two seconds of time that I could keep myself so, yet it relieved me greatly, gave me breath and new courage. I was covered again with water a good while, but not so long but I held it out; and finding the water had spent itself and began to return, I struck forward against the return of the waves, and felt ground again with my feet. I stood still a few moments to recover breath, and till the water went from me, and then took to my heels and ran with what strength I had farther towards the shore. But neither would this deliver me from the fury of the sea, which came pouring in after me again, and twice more I was lifted up by the waves and carried forwards as before, the shore being very flat.

Now as the waves were not so high as at first, being near land, I held my breath till the wave abated, and then fetched another run, which brought me so near the shore, that the next wave, though it went over me, yet did not so swallow me up as to carry me away; and the next run I took I got to the mainland, where, to my great comfort, I clambered on the cliffs of the shore and sat me down upon the grass, free from danger, and quite out of the reach of the water.

I cast my eyes to the stranded vessel, when the breach and froth of the sea being so big, I could hardly see it, it lay so far off, and considered, "Lord, how was it possible I could get on shore?"

After I had solaced my mind with the comfortable part of my condition, I began to look round me to see what kind of place I was in, and what was next to be done, and I soon found my comforts abate, and that, in a word, I had a dreadful deliverance; for I was wet, had no clothes to shift me, nor anything either to eat or drink to comfort me, neither did I see any prospect before me but that of perishing with hunger, or being devoured by wild beasts. And that which was particularly afflicting to me was, that I had no weapon either to hunt and kill any creature for my sustenance, or to defend myself against any other creature that might desire to kill me for theirs; — in a word, I had nothing about me but a knife, a tobacco-pipe, and a little tobacco in a box.

All the remedy that offered to my thoughts at that time was, to get up into a thick bushy tree like a fir, but thorny, which grew near me, and where I resolved to sit all night, and consider the next day what death I should die; for as yet I saw no prospect of life. I walked about a furlong from the shore to see if I could find any fresh water to drink, which I did, to my great joy; and having drunk, and put a little tobacco in my mouth to prevent hunger, I went to the tree, and getting up into it, endeavoured to place myself so as that if I should sleep I might not fall; and having cut me a short stick like a truncheon for my defence, I took up my lodging, and having been excessively fatigued, I fell fast asleep, and slept as comfortably as, I believe, few could have done in my condition, and found myself the most refreshed with it than I think I ever was on such an occasion.

CHAPTER THREE

When I waked it was broad day, the weather clear, and the storm abated, so that the sea did not rage and swell as before; but that which surprised me most was, that the ship was lifted off in the night from the sand where she lay by the swelling of the tide, and was driven up almost as far as the rock; this being within about a mile from the shore, where I was, and the ship seeming to stand upright still, I wished myself on board, that at least I might have some necessary things for my use.

A little after noon I found the sea very calm and the tide ebbed so far out that I could come within a quarter of a mile of the ship. And here I found a fresh renewing of my grief; for I saw evidently that if we had kept on board we had been all safe — that is to say, we had all got safe on shore, and I had not been so miserable as to be left entirely destitute of all comfort and company as I now was. This forced tears from my eyes again, but as there was little relief in that, I resolved, if possible, to get to the ship; so I pulled off my clothes, for the weather was hot to extremity, and took to the water. But when I came to the ship, my difficulty was still greater to know how to get on board; for as she lay aground and high out of the water, there was nothing within my reach to lay hold of. I swam round her twice, and the second time I spied a small piece of a rope, which I wondered if I did not see at first, hang down by the forechains so low as that with great difficulty I got hold of it, and by the help of that rope got up into the forecastle of the ship. Here I found that the ship had a great deal of water in her hold, but that she lay so on the side of a bank of hard sand, or rather earth, and her stern lay lifted up upon the bank, and her head low, almost to the water. By this means all her quarter was free, and all that was in that part was dry; for you may be sure my first work was to search and to see what was spoiled and what was free. And first I found that all the ship's provisions were dry and untouched by the water, and being very well disposed to eat, I went to the bread-room and filled my pockets with biscuit, and ate it as I went about other things, for I had no time to lose. I also found some rum in the great cabin, of which I took a large dram, and which I had indeed need enough of to spirit me for what was before me. Now I wanted nothing but a boat to furnish myself with many things which I foresaw would be very necessary to me.

It was in vain to sit still and wish for what was not to be had, and this extremity roused my application. We had several spare yards, and two or three large spars of wood, and a spare top-mast or two in the ship. I resolved to fall to work with these. and flung as many of them overboard as I could manage of their weight, tying every one with a rope that they might not drive away. When this was done, I went down the ship's side, and pulling them to me, I tied four of them fast together at both ends as well as I could, in the form of a raft, and laying two or three short pieces of plank upon them crossways, I found I could walk upon it very well, but that it was not able to bear any great weight, the pieces being too light. So I went to work, and with the carpenter's saw I cut a spare top-mast into three lengths, and added them to my raft, with a great deal of labour and pains; but hope of furnishing myself with necessaries encouraged me to go beyond what I should have been able to have done upon another occasion.

My raft was now strong enough to bear any reasonable weight. My next care was what to load it with, and how to preserve what I laid upon it from the surf of the sea. But I was not long considering this. I first laid all the planks or boards upon it that I could get, and having considered well what I most wanted, I first got three of the seamen's chests, which I had broken open and emptied, and lowered them down upon my raft. The first of these I filled with provisions — namely, bread, rice, three Dutch cheeses, five pieces of dried goat's flesh, which we lived much upon, and a little remainder of European corn which had been laid by for some fowls which we brought to sea with us; but the fowls were killed. There had been some barley and wheat together, but to my great disappointment I found afterwards that the rats had eaten or spoiled it all. As for liquors I found several cases of bottles belonging to our skipper, in which were some cordial waters. These I stowed by themselves, there being no need to put them into the chest, nor no room for them.

While I was doing this I found the tide began to flow, though very calm, and I had the mortification to see my coat, shirt and waistcoat, which I had left on shore upon the sand, swim away; as for my breeches, which were only linen and open-kneed, I swam on board in them and my stockings; however, this put me upon rummaging for clothes, of which I found enough, but took no more than I wanted for present use, for I had other things which my eye was more upon — as, first, tools to work with on shore, and it was after long searching that I found out the carpenter's chest, which was indeed a very useful prize to me, and much more valuable than a ship loading of gold would have been at that time. I got it down to my raft even whole as it was, without losing time to look into it, for I knew in general what it contained.

My next care was for some ammunition and arms. There were two very good fowling-pieces in the great cabin, and two pistols; these I secured first, with some powder-horns, and a small bag of shot, and two old rusty swords. I knew there were three barrels of powder in the ship, but knew not where our gunner had stowed them; but with much search I found them, two of them dry and good, the third had taken water. Those two I got to my raft with the arms; and now I thought myself pretty well freighted, and began to think how I should get to shore with them, having neither sail, oar, nor rudder, and the least capful of wind would have upset all my navigation.

I had three encouragements — first, a smooth calm sea; second, the tide rising and setting in to the shore; third, what little wind there was blew me towards the land. And thus, having found two or three broken oars belonging to the boat, and besides the tools which were in the chest, I found two saws, an axe, a hammer, and with this cargo, I put to sea. For a mile or thereabouts my raft went very well, only that I found it drive a little distant from the place where I had landed before; by which I perceived that there was some indraught of the water, and consequently I hoped to find some creek or river there, which I might make use of as a port to get to land with my cargo.

As I imagined, so it was. There appeared before me a little opening of the land, and I found a strong current of the tide set into it; so I guided my raft as well as I could to keep in the middle of the stream. But here I had like to have suffered a second shipwreck, which if I had, I think verily would have broken my hreat; for, knowing nothing of the coast, my raft ran aground at one end of it upon a shoal, and not being aground at the other end, it wanted but a little that all my cargo had slipped off towards that end that was afloat, and so fallen into the water. I did my utmost by setting my back against the chests, to keep them in their places, but could not thrust off the raft with all my strength, neither durst I stir from the posture I was in, but holding up the chests with all my might, stood in that manner near half an hour, in which time the rising of the water brought me a little more upon a level; and a little later, the water still rising, my raft floated again, and I thrust her off with the oar I had into the channel, and then driving up higher, I at length found myself in the mouth of a little river, with land on both sides, and a strong current or tide running up. I looked on both sides for a proper place to get to shore, for I was not willing to be driven too high up the river, hoping in time to see some ship at sea, and therefore resolved to place myself as near the coast as I could.

At length I spied a little cove on the right shore of the creek, to which with great pain and difficulty I guided my raft, and at last got so near as that, reaching ground with my oar, I could thrust her directly in. But here I had like to have dipped all my cargo in the sea again; for that shore lying pretty steep — that is to say, sloping — there was no place to land, but where one end of my float if it ran on shore, would lie so high, and the other sink lower than before, that it would endanger my cargo again. All that I could do was to wait until the tide was at the highest, keeping the raft with my oar like an anchor to hold the side of it fast to the shore near a flat piece of ground, which I expected the water would flow over; and so it did. As soon as I found water enough — for my raft drew about a foot of water — I thrust her on upon that flat piece of ground, and there fastened or moored her by sticking my two broken oars into the ground, one on one side near one end, and one on the other side near the other end; and thus I lay till the water ebbed away, and left my raft and all my cargo safe on shore.

My next work was to view the country, and seek a proper place for my habitation, and where to stow my goods to secure them from whatever might happen. Where I was I yet knew not, whether on the continent or on an island, whether inhabited or not inhabited, whether in danger of wild beasts or not. There was a hill not above a mile from me, which rose up very steep and high, and which seemed to overtop some other hills which lay as in a ridge from its northward. I took out one of the fowling-pieces and one of the pistols, and a horn of powder, and thus armed I travelled for discovery up to the top of that hill, where, after I had with great labour and difficulty got to the top, I saw my fate to my great affliction — namely, that I was in an island environed every way with the sea, no land to be seen, except some rocks which lay a great way off, and two small islands, less than this, which lay about three leagues to the west.

I found also that the island I was in was barren, and, as I saw good reason to believe, uninhabited, except by wild beasts — of whom, however, I saw none ; yet I saw abundance of fowls, but knew not their kinds, neither when I killed them could I tell what was fit for food, and what not. At my coming back, I shot at a great bird which I saw sitting upon a tree on the side of a great wood. I believe it was the first gun that had been fired there since the creation of the world. I had no sooner fired, but from all parts of the wood there arose an innumerable number of fowls of many sorts, making a confused screaming, and crying everyone according to his usual note; but not one of them of any kind that I knew. As for the creature I killed, I took it to be a kind of hawk, its colour and beak resembling it, but had no talons or claws more than common; its flesh was carrion and fit for nothing.

Contented with this discovery, I came back to my raft, and fell to work to bring my cargo on shore, which took me up the rest of that day. And what to do with myself at night I knew not, nor indeed where to rest; for I was afraid to lie down on the ground, not knowing but some wild beast might devour me, though, as I afterwards found, there was really no need for those fears.

However, as well as I could, I barricaded myself round with the chests and boards that I had brought on shore, and made a kind of hut for that night's lodging. As for food, I yet saw not which way to supply myself, except that I had seen two or three creatures like hares run out of the wood where I shot the fowl.

I now began to consider that I might yet get a great many things out of the ship which would be useful to me, and particularly some of the rigging and sails, and such other things as might come to land; and I resolved to make another voyage on board the vessel, if possible; and as I knew that the first storm that blew must necessarily break her all in pieces, I resolved to set all other things apart, till I got everything out of the ship that I could get. Then I called a council — that is to say, in my thoughts — whether I should take back the raft; but this appeared impracticable. So I resolved to go as before, when the tide was down; and I did so, only that I stripped before I went from my hut, having nothing on but a checkered shirt, and a pair of linen drawers, and a pair of pumps on my feet. I got on board the ship as before, and prepared a second raft; and having had experience of the first, I neither made this so unwieldy nor loaded it so hard, but yet I brought away several things very useful to me. At first, in the carpenter's stores, I found two or three bags full of nails and spikes, a great screwjack, a dozen or two of hatchets, and, above all, that most useful thing called a grindstone. All these I secured together, with several things belonging to the gunner, particularly two or three iron crows, and two barrels of musket bullets, seven muskets, and another fowling-piece, with some small quantity of powder more, a large bag full of small shot, and a great roll of sheet lead. But this last was so heavy I could not hoist it up to get it over the ship's side.

Besides these things, I took all the men's clothes that I could find, and a spare fore-topsail, a hammock, and some bedding; and with this I loaded my second raft, and brought them all safe on shore, to my very great comfort.

I was under some apprehensions during my absence from the land that at least my provisions might be devoured on shore; but when I came back I found no sign of any visitor, only there sat a creature like a wild cat upon one of the chests, which, when I came towards it, ran away a little distance, and then stood still. She sat very composed and unconcerned, and looked full in my face, as if she had a mind to be acquainted with me. I presented my gun at her, but as she did not understand it, she was perfectly unconcerned at it, nor did she offer to stir away. Upon which I tossed her a bit of biscuit — though, by the way, I was not very free of it, for my store was not great. However, I spared her a bit, I say, and she went to it, smelled of it, and ate it, and looked, as pleased, for more; but I thanked her, and could spare no more. So she marched off.

Having got my second cargo on shore, though I was fain to open the barrels of powder, and bring them by parcels — for they were too heavy, being large casks — I went to work to make me a little tent with the sail and some poles which I cut for that purpose; and into this tent, I brought everything that I knew would spoil either with rain or sun, and I piled all the empty chests and casks up in a circle round the tent, to fortify it from any sudden attempt either from man or beast.

When I had done this, I blocked up the door of the tent with some boards within, and an empty chest set up on end without, and spreading one of the beds upon the gound, laying my two pistols just at my head, and my gun at length by me, I went to bed for the first time, and slept very quietly all night, for I was very weary and heavy; for the night before I had slept little, and had laboured very hard all day, as well to fetch all those things from the ship as to get them on shore.

I had the biggest magazine of all kinds now that ever were laid up, I believe, for one man; but I was not satisfied still, for while the ship sat upright in that posture, I thought I ought to get everything out of her that I could; so every day at low water I went on board, and brought away something or other. But particularly the third time I went I brought away as much of the rigging as I could, as also all the small ropes and rope-twine I could get, with a piece of spare canvas, which was to mend the sails upon occasion, the barrel of wet gunpowder; in a word, I brought away all the sails first and last, only that I was fain to cut them in pieces, and bring as much at a time as I could, for they were no more useful to be sails, but as mere canvas only.

But that which comforted me more still was, that at last of all, after I had made five or six such voyages as these, and thought I had nothing more to expect from the ship that was worth my meddling with — I say, after all this, I found a great hogshead of biscuits, and three large runlets of rum or spirits, and a box of sugar, and a barrel of fine flour. This was surprising to me, because I had given over expecting any more provisions, except what was spoiled by the water. I soon emptied the hogshead, and, in a word, I got all this safe on shore also.

The next day, I made another voyage, and now having plundered the ship of what was portable and fit to hand out, I began with the cables; and cutting the great cable into pieces such as I could move, I got two cables and a hawser on shore, with all the ironwork I could get; and having cut down the spritsail yard, and the mizzen-yard, and everything I could to make a large raft, I loaded it with all those heavy goods, and came away. But my good luck began now to leave me; for this raft was so unwieldy and so overloaded that after I was entered the little cove where I had landed the rest of my goods, not being able to guide it so handily as I did the other, it overset, and threw me and all my cargo into the water. As for myself, it was no great harm, for I was near the shore; but as to my cargo, it was great part of it lost, especially the iron, which I expected would have been of great use to me. However, when the tide was out, I got most of the pieces of cable ashore and some of the iron, though with infinite labour: for I was fain to dip for it into the water, a work which fatigued me very much. After this I went every day on board, and brought away what I could get.

it. This cost me a great deal of time and labour, especially to cut the piles in the woods, bring them to the place, and drive them into the earth.

The entrance to this place I made to be, not by a door, but by a short ladder to go over the top; which ladder, when I was in, I lifted over after me. And so I was completely fenced in and fortified, as I thought, from all the world, and consequently slept secure in the night, which otherwise I could not have done; though, as it appeared afterward, there was no need of all this caution from the enemies that I apprehended danger from.

Into this fence or fortress, with infinite labour, I carried all my riches, all my provisions, ammunition, and stores, of which you have the account above. And I made me a large tent, which to preserve me from the rains that in one part of the year are very violent there, I made double — namely one smaller tent within, and one larger tent above it, and covered the uppermost with a large tarpaulin which I had saved among the sails.

And now I lay no more for a while in the bed which I had brought on shore, but in a hammock; which was indeed a very good one, and belonged to the mate of the ship.

Into this tent I brought all my provisions and everything that would spoil by the wet; and having thus enclosed all my goods I made up the entrance, which till now I had left open, and so passed and repassed, as I said, by a short ladder.

When I had done this, I began to work my way into the rock, and bringing all the earth and stones that I dug down out through my tent, I laid them up within my fence in the nature of a terrace, that

CHAPTER FOUR

I had been now thirteen days on shore, and had been eleven times on board the ship, in which time I had brought away all that one pair of hands could well be supposed capable to bring; though I believe verily, had the calm weather held, I should have brought away the whole ship piece by piece. But preparing the twelfth time to go on board, I found the wind begin to rise. However, at low water I went on board; and though I thought I had rummaged the cabin so effectually as that nothing more could be found, yet I discovered a locker with drawers in it, in one of which I found two or three razors and one pair of large scissors, with some ten or a dozen of good knives and forks; in another I found about thirty-six pounds value in money, some European coin, some Brazil, some pieces of eight, some gold, some silver.

I smiled to myself at the sight of this money. "Oh drug!" said I aloud, "what art thou good for? Thou art not worth to me, no not the taking off of the ground; one of those knives is worth all this heap. I have no manner of use for thee; even remain where thou art, and go to the bottom as a creature whose life is not worth saving." However, upon second thoughts, I took it away, and wrapping all this in a piece of canvas, I began to think of making another raft; but while I was preparing this, I found the sky overcast, and the wind began to rise, and in a quarter of an hour it blew a fresh gale from the shore. It presently occurred to me that it was in vain to pretend to make a raft with the wind off shore, and that it was my business to be gone before the tide of flood began, otherwise I might not be able to reach shore at all. Accordingly, I let myself down into the water, and swam across the channel which lay between the ship and the sands, and even that with difficulty enough, partly with the weight of the things I had about me, and partly the roughness of the water, for the wind rose very hastily, and before it was quite high water, it blew a storm.

But I was gotten home to my little tent, where I lay with all my wealth about me very secure. It blew very hard all that night; and in the morning when I looked out, behold, no more ship was to be seen! I was a little surprised, but recovered myself with this satisfactory reflection, namely, that I had lost no time nor abated any diligence to get everything out of her that could be useful to me, and that indeed there was little left in her that I was able to bring away, if I had had more time.

My thoughts were now wholly employed about securing myself against either savages, if any should appear, or wild beasts, if any were in the island; and I had many thoughts of the method how to do this, and what kind of dwelling to make, whether I should make me a cave in the earth, or a tent upon the earth. And, in short, I resolved upon both, the manner and description of which it may not be improper to give an account of.

I soon found the place I was in was not for my settlement, particularly because it was upon a low moorish ground near the sea, and, I believed, could not be wholesome, and more particulary, because there was no fresh water near it; so I resolved to find a more healthy and more convenient spot of ground.

In search of a place proper for this, I fou little plain on the side of a rising hill, whose towards this little plain was steep as a house-so that nothing could come down upon me from top. On the side of this rock there was a h place worn a little way in like the entrance or of a cave; but there was not really any ca way into the rock at all.

On the flat of the green, just before this h place, I resolved to pitch my tent. This plain not above a hundred yards broad, and about as long, and lay like a green before my door at the end of it descended irregularly every down into the low grounds by the sea-side. I on the north-north-west side of the hill, so was sheltered from the heat every day till it ca a west and by south sun, or thereabouts, wh those countries is near the setting.

Before I set up my tent, I drew a half before the hollow place, which took in abo yards in its semi-diameter from the rock, and yards in its diameter from its beginning and e

In this half-circle I pitched two rows of stakes, driving them into the ground till the very firm like piles, the biggest end being the ground about five foot and a half, and sha on the top. The two rows did not stand ab inches from one another.

Then I took the pieces of cable which I in the ship, and laid them in rows one upon within the circle, between these two rows of up to the top, placing other stakes in the leaning aginst them, about two foot and a h like a spur to a post; and this fence was s that neither man nor beast could get into it so it raised the ground within about a foot and a half; and thus I made me a cave just behind my tent, which served me like a cellar to my house.

It cost me much labour and many days before all these things were brought to perfection, and therefore I must go back to some other things which took up some of my thoughts. At the same time it happened after I had laid my scheme for the setting up my tent, and making the cave, that a storm of rain falling from a thick, dark cloud, a sudden flash of lightning happened, and after that a great clap of thunder, as is naturally the effect of it. I was not so much surprised with the lightning as I was with a thought which darted into my mind as swift as the lightning itself — O my powder! My heart sunk within me when I thought that at one blast all my powder might be destroyed, on which not my defence only, but the providing me food, as I thought, entirely depended. I was nothing near so anxious about my own danger though had the powder taken fire, I had never known who had hurt me.

Such impression did this make upon me, that after the storm was over I laid aside all my works, my building and fortifying, and applied myself to make bags and boxes to separate the powder and keep it a little and a little in a parcel, in hope that whatever might come it might not all take fire at once, and to keep it so apart that it should not be possible to make one part fire another. I finished this work in about a fortnight; and I think my powder, which in all was about two hundred and forty pounds weight, was divided in not less than a hundred parcels.

And now I begin to enter into a melancholy relation of a scene of silent life, such, perhaps, as was never heard of in the world before. I shall take it from its beginning, and continue it in its order. It was, by my account, the 30th September when, in the manner as above said, I first set foot upon this horrid island, when the sun being, to us, in its autumnal equinox, was almost just over my head; for I reckoned myself, by observation, to be in the latitudine of 9 degrees 22 minutes north of the line.

After I had been there about ten or twelve days, it came into my thoughts that I should lose my reckoning of time for want of books and pen and ink, and should even forget the Sabbath days from the working days; but, to prevent this, I cut it with my knife upon a large post, in capital letters, and making it into a great cross, I set it up on the shore where I first landed — namely, I CAME ON SHORE HERE ON THE 30th OF SEPTEMBER, 1659. Upon the sides of this square post I cut every day a notch with my knife and every seventh notch was as long again as the rest, and every first day of the month as long again as that long one, and thus I kept my calendar, or weekly, monthly, and yearly reckoning of time.

In the next place we are to observe, that among the many things which I brought out of the ship in the several voyages which, as above mentioned, I made to it, I got several things of less value, but not all less useful to me, which I omitted setting down before; as, in particular, pens, ink, and paper, several parcels in the captain's, mate's, gunner's, and carpenter's keeping, three or four compasses, some mathematical instruments, dials, perspectives, charts and books of navigation; all which I huddled together, whether I might want them or no. Also, I found three very good Bibles, which came to me in my cargo from England, and which I had packed up among my things; some Portuguese books also I found, and among them two or three prayer-books, and several other books: all which I carefully secured. And I must not forget that we had in the ship a dog and two cats, of whose eminent history I may have occasion to say something in its place, for I carried both the cats with me; and as for the dog, he jumped out of the ship of himself, and swam on shore to me the day after I went on shore with my first cargo, and was a trusty servant to me many years. I wanted nothing that he could fetch me, nor any company that he could make up to me; I only wanted to have him talk to me, but that he would not do. As I observed before, I found pen, ink and paper, and I husbanded them to the utmost; and I shall show that, while my ink lasted, I kept things very exact; but after that was gone I could not, for I could not make any ink by any means that I could device.

And this put me in mind that I wanted many things, notwithstanding all that I had amassed together; and of these, this of ink was one; as also spade, pick-axe, and shovel, to dig or remove the earth; needles, pins, and thread; as for linen, I soon learned to want that without much difficulty.

This want of tools made every work I did go on heavily, and I was near a whole year before I had entirely finished my little pale or surrounded habitation. The piles or stakes, which were as heavy as I could well lift, were a long time in cutting and preparing in the woods, and more by far in bringing home; so that I spent sometimes two days in cutting and bringing home one of those posts, and a third day in driving it into the ground: for which purpose I got a heavy piece of wood at first, but at last bethought myself of one of the iron crows; which, however, though I found it, yet it made driving those posts or piles very laborious and tedious work.

But what need I have been concerned at the tediousness of anything I had to do, seeing I had time enough to do it in, nor had I any other employment, if that had been over, at least that I could foresee, except the ranging the island to seek for food, which I did more or less every day.

I have already described my habitation, which was a tent upon the side of a rock, surrounded with a strong pale of posts and cables; but I might now rather call it a wall, for I raised a kind of wall up against it of turfs, about two foot thick on the outside; and after some time, I think it was a year and a half, I raised rafters from it leading to the rock, and thatched or covered it with boughs of trees, and such things as I could get to keep out the rain, which I found at some times of the year very violent.

I have already observed how I brought all my goods into this pale, and into the cave which I had made behind me; but I must observe, too, that at first this was a confused heap of goods, which, as they lay in no order, so they took up all my place. I had no room to turn myself, so I set myself to enlarge my cave and works farther into the earth; for it was a loose sandy rock, which yielded easily to the labour I bestowed upon it; and so, when I found I was pretty safe as to beasts of prey, I worked sideways to the right hand into the rock;

and then, turning to the right again, worked quite out, and made me a door to come out, on the outside of my pale or fortification.

This gave me not only egress and regress, as it were, a back way to my tent and to my storehouse, but gave me room to stow my goods.

And now I began to apply myself to make such necessary things as I found I most wanted, as particularly a chair and table; for without those I was not able to enjoy the few comforts I had in the world — I could not write or eat, or do several things with so much pleasure without a table.

So I went to work; and here I must needs observe, that as reason is the substance and original of the mathematics, so by starting and squaring everything by reason, and by making the most rational judgement of things, every man may be in time master of every mechanic art. I had never handled a tool in my life, and yet in time, by labour, application, and contrivance, I found at last that I wanted nothing but I could have made it, especially if I had had tools; however, I made abundance of things, even without tools, and some with no more tools than an adze and a hatchet, which perhaps were never made that way before, and that with infinite labour. For example, if I wanted a board, I had no other way but to cut down a tree, set it on an edge before me, and hew it flat on either side with my axe, till I had brought it to be thin as a plank, and theh dub it smooth with my adze. It is true, by this method I could make but one board out of a whole tree, but this I had no remedy for but patience, any more than I had for the prodigious deal of time and labour which it took me up to make a plank or board. But my time and labour was little worth, and so it was as well employed one way as another.

However, I made me a table and a chair, as I observe above, in the first place, and this I did out of the short pieces of boards that I brought on my raft from the ship. But when I had wrought out some boards, as above, I made large shelves of the breadth of a foot and a half one over another, all along one side of my cave, to lay all my tools, nails, and ironwork and, in a word, to separate everything at large in their places, that I might come easily at them. I knocked pieces into the wall of the rock to hang my guns and all things that would hang up.

So that had my cave been to be seen, it looked like a general magazine of all necessary things; and I had everything so ready at my hand that it was a great pleasure to me to see all my goods in such order, and especially to find my stock of all necessaries so great.

CHAPTER FIVE

And now it was when I began to keep a journal of every day's employment — for indeed at first I was in too much hurry, and not only hurry as to labour, but in too much discomposure of mind — and my journal would have been full of many dull things. For example, I must have said thus: — September 30. After I got to shore and had escaped drowning, instead of being thankful to God for my deliverance — having first vomited with the great quantity of salt water which was gotten into my stomach, and recovering myself a little — I ran about the shore, wringing my hands and beating my head and face, exclaiming at my misery, and crying out I was undone, undone! till, tired and faint, I was forced to lie down on the ground to repose, but durst not sleep for fear of being devoured.

Some days after this, and after I had been on board the ship and got all that I could out of her, yet I could not forbear getting up to the top of a little mountain and looking out to sea in hopes of seeing a ship, then fancy at a vast distance I spied a sail, please myself with the hopes of it, and then after looking steadily till I was almost blind, lose it quite, and sit down and weep like a child, and thus increase my misery by my folly.

But having gotten over these things in some measure, and having settled my household stuff and habitation, made me a table and a chair, and all as handsome about me as I could, I began to keep my journal, of which I shall here give you the copy (though in it will be told all these particulars over again) as long as it lasted, for, having no more ink, I was forced to leave it off.

THE JOURNAL

September 30, 1659. I, poor, miserable Robinson Crusoe, being shipwrecked during a dreadful storm in the offing, came on shore on this dismal unfortunate island, which I called the Island of Despair, all the rest of the ship's company being drowned, and myself being dead.

All the rest of that day I spent in afflicting myself at the dismal circumstances I was brought to — namely, I had neither food, house, clothes, weapon, nor place to fly to, and, in despair of any relief, saw nothing but death before me — either that I should be devoured by wild beasts, murdered by savages, or starved to death for want of food. At the approach of night I slept in a tree for fear of wild creatures, but slept soundly though it rained all night.

October I. In the morning I saw, to my great surprise, the ship had floated with the high tide, and was driven on shore again much nearer the island; which as it was some comfort, on one hand, for, seeing her sit upright, and not broken to pieces, I hoped, if the wind abated, I might get on board and get some food and necessaries out of her for my relief; so, on the other hand, it renewed my grief at the loss of my comrades who, I imagined, if we had all stayed on board, might have been saved the ship, or at least that they would not have been all drowned as they were, and that had the men been saved, we might perhaps have built us a boat out of the ruins of the ship to have carried us to some other part of the world. I spent great part of this day in perplexing myself on these things; but at length, seeing the ship almost dry, I went upon the sand as near as I could, and then swam on board; this day also it continued raining, though with no wind at all.

From the 1st of October to the 24 th. All these days entirely spent in many several voyages to get all I could out of the ship, which I brought on shore, every tide of flood, upon rafts. Much rain also in these days, though with some intervals of fair weather; but, it seems, this was the rainy season.

October 20. I overset my raft, and all the goods I had got upon it; but being in shoal water, and the things being chiefly heavy, I recovered many of them when the tide was out.

October 25. It rained all night and all day, with some gusts of wind, during which time the ship broke in pieces, the wind blowing a little harder than before, and was no more to be seen, except the wreck of her, and that only at low water. I spent this day in covering and securing the goods which I had saved, that the rain might not spoil them.

October 26. I walked about the shore almost all day to find out a place to fix my habitation, greatly concerned to secure myself from an attack in the night either from wild beasts or men. Towards night I fixed upon a proper place under a rock, and marked out a semi circle of my encampment, which I resolved to strengthen with a work, wall, or fortification made of double piles, lined within with cables and without with turf.

From the 26th to the 30th I worked very hard in carrying all my goods to my new habitation, though some part of the time it rained exceeding hard.

The 31 st in the morning I went out into the island with my gun to see for some food, and discover the country, when I killed a she-goat, and her kid followed me home, which I afterwards killed also, because it would not feed.

November 1. I set up my tent under a rock, and lay there for the first night, making it as large as I could with stakes driven in to swing my hammock upon.

November 2. I set up all my chests and boards, and the pieces of timber which made my rafts, and with them formed a fence round me, a little within the place I had marked out for my fortification.

November 3. I went out with my gun, and killed two fowls like ducks, which were very good food. In the afternoon went to work to make me a table.

November 4. This morning I began to order my times of work, of going out with my gun, time of sleep and time of diversion — namely, every morning I walked out with my gun for two or three hours if it did not rain, then employed myself to work till about eleven o'clock, then ate what I had to live on; and from twelve to two I lay down to sleep, the weather being excessive hot; and then in the evening to work again. The working part of this day and of the next were wholly employed in making my table; for I was yet but a very sorry workman, though time and necessity made me a complete natural mechanic soon after, as I believe it would do any one else.

November 5. This day I went abroad with my gun and my dog, and killed a wild cat, her skin pretty soft, but her flesh good for nothing. Every creature I killed I took off the skins and preserved them. Coming back by the sea-shore, I saw many sorts of sea-fowls which I did not understand; but was surprised and almost frightened with two or three seals, which while I was gazing at, not well knowing what they were, got into the sea, and escaped me for that time.

November 6. After my morning walk I went to work with my table again, and finished it, though not to my liking; nor was it long before I learned to mend it.

November 7. Now it began to be settled fair weather. The 7th, 8th, 9th, 10th, and part of the 12th (for the 11th was Sunday), I took wholly up to make me a chair, and with much ado brought it to a tolerable shape, but never to please me; and even in the making I pulled it to pieces several times. **Note.** — I soon neglected my keeping Sundays; for, omitting my mark for them on my post, I forgot which was which.

November 13. This day it rained, which refreshed me exceedingly, and cooled the earth; but it was accompanied with terrible thunder and lightning, which frightened me dreadfully for fear of my powder. As soon as it was over I resolved to separate my stock of powder; and so that it might not be in danger.

November 14, 15, 16. These three days I spent in making little square chests or boxes, which might hold about a pound, or two pounds at most, of powder; and so putting the powder in, I stowed it in places as secure and remote from one another as possible. On one of these three days I killed a large bird that was good to eat, but I know not what to call it.

November 17. This day I began to dig behind my tent into the rock, to make room for my farther conveniency. **Note** — Three things I wanted exceedingly for this work, namely, a pick-axe, a shovel, and a wheelbarrow or basket. So I desisted from my work, and began to consider how to supply that want, and make me some tools. As for a pick-axe I made use of the iron crows, which were proper enough though heavy. But the next thing was a shovel or spade; this was so absolutely necessary, that indeed I could do nothing effectually without it. But what kind of one to make I knew not.

November 18. The next day, in searching the woods, I found a tree of that wood, or like it, which in the Brazils they call the iron tree, for its exceeding hardness. On this, with great labour and almost spoiling my axe, I cut a piece, and brought it home too with difficulty enough, for it was exceeding heavy.

The excessive hardness of the wood, and having no other way, made me a long while upon this machine; for I worked it effectually by little and little into the form of a shovel or spade, the handle exactly shaped like ours in England, only that the broad part having no iron shod upon it at bottom, it would not last me so long. However, it served well enough for the uses which I had occasion to put it to; but never was a shovel, I believe, made after that fashion, or so long a-making.

I was still deficient, for I wanted a basket or a wheelbarrow. A basket I could not make by any means, having no such things as twigs that would bend to make wicker ware, at least none yet found out. And as to a wheelbarrow, I fancied I could make all but the wheel, but that I had no notion of, neither did I know how to go about it; besides, I had no posible way to make the iron gudgeons for the spindle or axis of the wheel to run in, so I gave it over. And so, for carrying away the earth which I dug out of the cave, I made me a thing like a hod, which the labourers carry mortar in when they serve the bricklayers.

This was not so difficult to me as the making the shovel; and yet this and the shovel, and the attempt which I made in vain to make a wheelbarrow, took me up no less than four days — I mean always excepting my morning walk with my gun, which I seldom failed, and very seldom failed also bringing home something fit to eat.

November 23. My other work having now stood still because of my making these tools, when they were finished I went on, and working every day as my strength and time allowed, I spent eighteen days entirely in widening and deepening my cave, that it might hold my goods commodiously.

Note. — During all this time I worked to make this room or cave spacious enough to accommodate me as a warehouse or magazine, a kitchen, a dining-room, and a cellar. As for my lodging, I kept to the tent, except that sometimes, in the wet season of the year, it rained so hard that I could not keep myself dry; which caused me afterwards to cover all my place within my pale with long poles in the form of rafters, leaning against the rock, and load them with flags and large leaves of trees like a thatch.

December 10. I began now to think my cave or vault finished, when on a sudden (it seems I had made it too large) a great quantity of earth fell down from the top and one side, so much that, in short, it frightened me; and not without reason too, for if I had been under it, I had never wanted a grave-digger. Upon this disaster I had a great deal of work to do over again; for I had the loose earth to carry out, and, which was of more importance, I had the ceiling to prop up, so that I might be sure no more would come down.

December 11. This day I went to work with it accordingly, and got two shores or posts pitched upright to the top, with two pieces of boards across over each post. This I finished the next day, and setting more posts up with boards, in about a week more I had the roof secured; and the posts, standing in rows, served me for partitions to part of my house.

December 17. From this day to the 20th I placed shelves, and knocked up nails on the posts to hang everything up that could be hung up; and now I began to be in some order within doors.

December 20. Now I carried everything into the cave and began to furnish my house, and set up some pieces of boards, like a dresser, to order my victuals upon; but boards began to be very scarce with me. Also I made me another table.

December 24. Much rain all night and all day. No stirring out.

December 25. Rain all day.

December 26. No rain, and the earth much cooler than before and pleasanter.

December 27. Killed a young goat, and lamed another so that I caught it, and led it home in a string. When I had it home I bound and splintered up its leg, which was broken. **N. B.** — I took such care of it that it lived, and the leg grew well and as strong as ever; but by my nursing it so long it grew tame, and fed upon the little green at my door, and would not go away. This was the first time that I entertained a thought of breeding up some tame creatures, that I might have food when my powder and shot was all spent.

December 28, 29, 30. Great heats and no breeze, so that there was no stirring abroad, except in the evening for food. Thus time I spent in putting all my things in order within doors.

January 1. Very hot still, but I went abroad early and late with my gun, and lay still in the middle of the day. This evening, going farther into the valleys which lay towards the centre of the island, I found there was plenty of goats, though exceeding shy and hard to come at. However, I resolved to try if I could not bring my dog to hunt them down.

January 2. Accordingly, the next day I went out with my dog and set him upon the goats; but I was mistaken, for they all faced about upon the dog and he knew his danger too well, for he would not come near them.

January 3. I began my fence or wall which, being still jealous of my being attacked by somebody, I resolved to make very thick and strong.

N. B. This wall being described before, I purposely omit what was said in the journal. It is sufficient to observe that I was no less time than from the 3rd of January to the 14th April working, finishing, and perfecting this wall, though it was no more than about twenty-four yards in length, being a half circle from one place in the rock to another place about eight yards from it the door of the cave being in the centre behind it.

All this time I worked very hard, the rains hindering me many days, nay, sometimes weeks together; but I thought I should never be perfectly secure till this wall was finished. And it is scarce credible what inexpressible labour everything was done with, especially the bringing piles out of the woods and driving them into the ground, for I made them much bigger than I need to have done.

When this wall finished, and the outside double fenced with a turf wall raised up close to it, I persuaded myself that if any people were to come, on shore there, they would not perceive anything like a habitation. And it was very well I did so, as may be observed hereafter upon a very remarkable occasion.

During this time I made my rounds in the woods for game every day when the rain admitted me, and made frequent discoveries in these walks of something or other to my advantage. Particularly I found a kind of wild pigeon, who built not as wood-pigeons, in a tree, but rather as house-pigeons in the holes of the rocks; and taking some young ones, I endeavoured to breed them up tame, and did so; but when they grew older they flew all away, which perhaps was at first for want of feeding them, for I had nothing to give them. However, I frequently found their nests, and got their young ones, which were very good meat.

And now, in the managing my household affairs, I found myself wanting in many things, which I thought at first was impossible for me to make, as indeed as to some of them it was. For instance, I could never make a cask to be hooped. I had a small runlet or two, as I observed before, but I could never arrive to the capacity of making one by them, though I spent many weeks about it. I could neither put in the heads, nor joint the staves so true to one another as to make them hold water. So I gave that also over.

In the next place, I was at a great loss for candles; so that as soon as ever it was dark, which was generally by seven o'clock, I was obliged to go to bed. I remembered the lump of beeswax with which I made candles in my African adventure, but I had none of that now. The only remedy I had was, that when I had killed a goat, I saved the tallow; and with a little dish made of clay, which I baked in the sun, to which I added a wick of some oakum, I made me a lamp, and this gave me light, though not a clear, steady light, like a candle. In the middle of all my labours it happened that, rummaging my things, I found a little bag, which, as I hinted before, had been filled with corn for the feeding of poultry, not for this voyage, but before, as I suppose, when the ship came from Lisbon. What little remainder of corn had been in the bag was all devoured with the rats, and I saw nothing in the bag husks and dust; and being willing to have the bag for some other use (I think it was to put powder in, when I divided it for fear of the lightning, or some such use), I shook the husks of corn out of it on one side of my fortification under the rock.

It was a little before the rains just now mentioned that I threw this stuff away, taking no notice of anything, and not so much as remembering that I had thrown anything there, when, about a month after, or thereabout, I saw some few stalks of something green shooting out of the ground, which I fancied might be some plant I had not seen; but I was surprised and perfectly astonished when, after a longer time, I saw about ten or twelve ears come out, which were perfect green barley, of the same kind as our European, nay as our English barley.

This touched my heart a little, and brought tears out of my eyes; and I began to bless myself that such a prodigy of nature should happen upon my account. And this was the more strange to me, because I saw near it still all along by the side of the rock some other straggling stalks, which proved to be stalks of rice, and which I knew because I had seen it grow in Africa when I was ashore there.

I carefully saved the ears of this corn, you may be sure, in their season, which was about the end of June; and laying up every corn, I resolved to sow them all again, hoping in time to have some quantity sufficient to supply me with bread. But it was not till the fourth year that I could allow myself the least grain of this corn to eat, and even then but sparingly, as I shall say afterwards in its order, for I lost all that I sowed the first season by not observing the proper time, for I sowed it just before the dry season, so that it never came up at all, at least not as it would have done — of which in its place.

Besides this barley, there was, as above, twenty or thirty stalks of rice, which I preserved with the same care, and whose use was of the same kind or to the same purpose — namely, to make my bread, or rather food, for I found ways to cook it up without baking, though I did that also after some time. But to return to my journal.

I worked excessively hard these three or four months to get my wall done; and the 14th April I close it up, contriving to go into it, not by a door, but over the wall by a ladder, that there might be no sign it the outside of my habitation.

April 16. I finished the ladder; so I went up with the ladder to the top, and then pulled it up after me, and let it down on the inside. This was a complete enclosure to me, for within I had room enough, and nothing could come at me from without unless it could first mount my wall.

The very next day after this wall was finished I had almost had all my labour overthrown at once, and myself killed. The case was thus: As I was busy in the inside of it, behind my tent, just in the entrance into my cave, I was terribly frightened with a most dreadful surprising thing indeed, for all of a sudden I found the earth come crumbling down from the roof of my cave and from the edge of the hill over my head, and two of the posts I had set up in the cave cracked in a frightful manner. I was heartily scared, but thought nothing of what was really the cause — only thinking that the top of my cave was falling in, as some of it had done before; and for fear I should be buried in it, I ran forward to my ladder, and not thinking myself safe there neither, I got over my wall for fear of the pieces of the hill which I expected might roll down upon me. I was no sooner stepped down upon the firm ground but I plainly saw it was a terrible earthquake, for the ground I stood on shook three times at about eight minutes' distance with three such shocks as would have overturned the strongest building that could be supposed to have stood on the earth; and a great piece of the top of a rock, which stood about half a mile from me next the sea, fell down with such a terrible noise as I never heard in all my life. I perceived also the very sea was put into violent motion by it, and I believe the shocks were stronger under the water than on the island.

I was so amazed with the thing itself — having never felt the like or discoursed with any one that had — that I was like one dead or stupefied; and the motion of the earth made my stomach sick, like one that was tossed at sea. But the noise of the falling of the rock awaked me, as it were, and rousing me from the stupefied condition I was in, filled me with horror, and I thought of nothing then but the hill falling upon my tent and all my household goods, and burying all at once; and this sunk my very soul within me a second time.

After the third shock was over, and I felt no more for some time. I began to take courage; and yet I had not heart enough to go over my wall again, for fear of being buried alive, but sat still upon the ground, greatly cast down and disconsolate, not knowing what to do. All this while I had not the least serious religious thought, nothing but the common "Lord have mercy upon me"; and when it was over, that went away too.

While I sat thus, I found the air overcast and grow cloudy, as if it would rain. Soon after that the wind rose by little and little, so that in less than half an hour it blew a most dreadful hurricane. The sea was all on a sudden covered over with foam and froth, the shore was covered with the breach of the water, the trees were torn up by the roots, and a terrible storm it was; and this held about three hours and then began to abate, and in two hours more it was calm and began to rain very hard.

This violent rain forced me to a new work — namely, to cut a hole through my new fortification like a sink to let the water go out, which would else have drowned my cave. After I had been in my cave some time and found still no more shocks of the earthquake follow, I began to be more composed; and now to support my spirits — which indeed wanted it very much — I went to my little store and took a small sup of rum, which however I did then and always very sparingly, knowing I could have no more when that was gone.

CHAPTER SIX

It continued raining all that night and great part of the next day, so that I could not stir abroad; but my mind being more composed, I began to think of what I had best do, concluding that if the island was subject to these earthquakes there would be no living for me in a cave, but I must consider of building me some little hut in an open place which I might surround with a wall as I had done here, and so make myself secure from wild beasts or men, but concludent, if I stayed where I was, I should certainly, one time or other, be buried alive.

With these thoughts I resolved to remove my tent from the place where it stood, which was just under the hanging precipice of the hill, and which, if it should be shaken again, would certainly fall upon my tent. And I spent the two next days, being the 19th and 20th of April, in contriving where and how to remove my habitation.

In the meantime, it occurred to me that it would require a vast deal of time for me to do this, and that I must be content to run the venture where I was, till I had formed a camp for myself, and had secured it so as to remove it. So with this resolution, I composed myself for a time, and resolved that I would go to work with all speed to build me a wall with piles and cables, & c. in a circle as before, and set my tent up in it when I was finished, but that I would venture to stay where I was till it was finished and fit to remove to. This was the 21st.

April 22. The next morning I began to consider of means to put this resolve in execution, but I was at a great loss about my tools. I had three large axes and abundance of hatchets (for we carried the hatchets for traffic with the Indians), but with much chopping and cutting knotty hard wood they were all full of notches and dull; and though I had a grindstone, I could not turn it and grind my tools too. This cost me as much thought as a statesman would have bestowed upon a grand point of politics, or a judge upon the life and death of a man. At length I contrived a wheel with a string to turn it with my foot, that I might have both my hands at liberty. **Note.** I had never seen any such thing in England, or at least not to take notice how it was done, though since I have observed it is very common there; besides that, my grindstone was very large and heavy. This machine cost me a full week's work to bring it to perfection.

April 28, 29. These two whole days I took up in grinding my tools, my machine for turning my grindstone performing very well.

April 30. Having perceived my bread had been low a great while, now I took a survey of it and reduced myself to one biscuit-cake a day, which made my heart very heavy.

May 1. In the morning, looking towards the sea-side, the tide being low, I saw something lie on the shore bigger than ordinary, and it looked like a cask. When I came to it, I found a small barrel and two or three pieces of the wreck of the ship, which were driven on shore by the late hurricane; and looking towards the wreck itself, I thought it seemed to lie higher out of the water than it used to do. I examined the barrel which was driven on shore, and soon found it was a barrel of gun-powder; but it had taken water and the powder was caked as hard as a stone. However, I rolled it farther on shore for the present, and went on upon the sands as near as I could to the wreck of the ship to look for more.

When I came down to the ship I found it strangely removed. The forecastle, which lay before buried in sand, was heaved up at least six foot; and the stern, which was broken to pieces and parted from the rest by the force of the sea soon after I had left rummaging her, was tossed, as it were, up and cast on one side. However, as I had learned not to despair of anything, I resolved to pull everything to pieces that I could of the ship, concluding that everything I could get from her would be of some use or other to me.

May 3. I began with my saw, and cut a piece of a beam through, which I thought held some of the upper part or quarter-deck together; and when I had cut it through I cleared away the sand as well as I could from the side which lay highest; but the tide coming in, I was obliged to give over for that time.

May 4. I went a-fishing, but caught not one fish that I durst eat of, till I was weary of my sport; when I was just going to leave off, I caught a young dolphin. I had made me a long line of some rope yarn, but I had no hooks, yet I frequently caught fish enough, as much as I cared to eat; all which I dried in the sun, and ate them dry.

May 5. Worked on the wreck, cut another beam asunder, and brought three great fir planks off from the decks, which I tied together, and made swim on shore when the tide of flood came on.

May 6. Worked hard on the wreck. Got several iron bolts out of her, and other pieces of iron-work, worked very hard, and came home very much tired, and had thoughts of giving it over.

May 7. Went to the wreck again, but with an intent not to work; but found the weight of the wreck had broken itself down, the beams being cut, that several pieces of the ship seemed to lie loose, and the inside of the hold lay so open that I could see into it, but almost full of water and sand.

May 8. Went to wreck, and carried an iron crow to wrench up the deck, which lay now quite clear of the water or sand. I wrenched open two planks, and brought them on shore also with the tide. I left the iron crow in the wreck for next day.

May 9. Went to the wreck, and with the crow made way into the body of the wreck, and felt several casks, and loosened them with the crow, but could not break them up. I felt also the roll of English lead, and could stir it, but it was too heavy to remove.

May, 10, 11, 12, 13, 14. Went every day to the wreck, and got a great deal of pieces of timber and boards, or planks, and two or three hundredweight of iron.

May 15. I carried two hatchets to try if I could not cut a piece off of the roll of lead, by placing the edge of one hatchet and driving it with the other; but as it lay about a foot and a half in the water, I could not make any blow to drive the hatchet.

May 16. It had blowed hard in the night, and the wreck appeared more broken by the force of the water; but I stayed so long in the woods to get pigeons for food, that the tide prevented me going to the wreck that day.

May 17. I saw some pieces of the wreck blown on shore, at a great distance, near two miles off me, but resolved to see what they were, and found it was a piece of the lead but too heavy for me to bring away.

May 24. Every day to this day I worked on the wreck, and with hard labour I loosened some things so much with the crow, that the first blowing tide several casks floated out, and two of the seamen's chests; but the wind blowing from the shore, nothing came to land that day but pieces of timber, and a hogs-head which had some Brazil pork in it, but the salt water and the sand had spoiled it.

I continued this work every day to the 15th June, except the time necessary to get food, which I always appointed, during this part of my employment, to be when the tide was up, that I might be ready when it was ebbed out; and by this time I had gotten timber and plank and iron-work enough to have built a good boat, if I had known how; and also, I got at several times and in several pieces, near one hundredweight of the sheet lead.

June 16. Going down to the seaside, I found a large tortoise or turtle. This was the first I had seen; which, it seems, was only my misfortune, not any defect of the place or scarcity; for had I happened to be on the other side of the island, I might have had hundreds of them every day, as I found afterwards; but, perhaps, had paid dear enough for them.

June 17. I spent in cooking the turtle. I found in her three score eggs; and her flesh was to me at that time the most savoury and pleasant that ever I tasted in my life, having had no flesh, but of goats and fowls, since I landed in this horrid place.

June 18. Rained all day, and I stayed within. I thought at this time the rain felt cold, and I was something chilly, which I knew was not usual in that latitude.

June 19. Very ill, and shivering, as if the weather had been cold.

June 20. No rest all night, violent pains in my head, and feverish.

June 21. Very ill. Frightened almost to death with the apprehensions of my sad condition — to be sick and no help. Prayed to God for the first time since the storm off Hull; but scarce knew what I said, or why, my thoughts being all confused.

June 22. A little better, but under dreadful apprehension of sickness.

June 23. Very bad again, cold and shivering, and then a violent headache.

June 24. Much better.

June 25. An ague, very violent. The fit held me seven hours, cold fit and hot, with faint sweats after it.

June 26. Better; and having no victuals to eat, took my gun, but found myself very weak. However, I killed a she-goat, and with much difficulty got it home, and broiled some of it and ate. I would fain have stewed it, and made some broth, but had no pot.

June 27. The ague again, so violent that I lay abed all day, and neither ate nor drank. I was ready to perish for thirst, but so weak, I had not strength to stand up or to get myself any water to drink. Prayed to God again; but was light headed, and when I was not, I was so ignorant that I knew not what to say; only I lay and cried, "Lord, look upon me; Lord, pity me; Lord, have mercy upon me!" I suppose I did nothing else for two or three hours, till the fit wearing off I fell asleep, and did not wake till far in the night. When I waked I found myself much refreshed, but weak and exceeding thirsty. However, as I had no water in my whole habitation, I was forced to lie till morning, and went to sleep again.

June 28. Having been somewhat refreshed with the sleep I had had, and the fit being entirely off, I got up; and though the fright and terror of my dream was very great, yet I considered that the fit of the ague would return again the next day, and now was the time to get something to refresh and support myself when I should be ill. And the first thing I did, I filled a large square case-bottle with water, and set it upon my table, in reach of my bed; and to take off the chill or aguish disposition of the water, I put about a quarter of a pint of rum into it and mixed them together. Then I got me a piece of the goat's flesh and broiled it on the coals, but could eat very little. I walked about, but was very weak, and withal very sad and heavy-hearted in the sense of my miserable condition, dreading the return of my distemper the next day. At night I made my supper of three of the turtle's eggs, which I roasted in the ashes, and ate, as we call it, in the shell: and this was the first bit of food I had ever asked God's blessing to, even as I could remember, in my whole life.

After I had eaten I tried to walk, but found myself so weak that I could hardly carry the gun (for I never went out without that); so I went but a little way, and sat down upon the ground, looking out upon the sea, which was just before me, and very calm and smooth.

Now as the apprehension of the return of my distemper terrified me very much, it occurred to my thought that the Brazilians take no physic but their tobacco for almost all distempers; and I had a piece of a roll of tobacco in one of the chests, which was quite cured, and some also that was green and not quite cured.

What use to make of the tobacco I knew not, as to my distemper, or whether it was good for it or no; But I tried several experiments with it, as if I was resolved it should hit one way or other. I first took a piece of a leaf and chewed it in my mouth, which indeed at first almost stupefied my brain, the tobacco being green and strong and that I had not been much used to it; then I took some and steeped it an hour or two in some rum, and resolved to take a dose of it when I lay down; and lastly I burned some upon a pan of coals, and held my nose close over the smoke of it as long as I could bear it, as well for the heat as almost for suffocation.

In the interval of this operation, I took up the Bible and began to read; but my head was too much disturbed with the tobacco to bear reading, at least that time. Only, having opened the book casually, the first words that occurred to me were these, "Call upon me in the day of trouble; I will deliver thee, and thou shalt glorify Me."

The words were very apt in my case, and made some impression upon my thoughts at the time of reading them, though not so much as they did afterwards; for, as for being delivered, the word had no sound, as I may say, to me; the thing was so remote, so impossible in my apprehension of things, that I began to say as the children of Israel did, when they were promised flesh to eat, "Can God spread a table in the wilderness?" so I began to say, "Can God Himself deliver me from this place?" and as it was not for many years that any hope appeared, this prevailed very often upon my thoughts; but, however, the words made a great impression upon me, and I mused upon them very often. It grew now late, and the tobacco had, as I said, dozed my head so much that I inclined to sleep; so I left my lamp burning in the cave lest I should want anything in the night, and went to bed; but before I lay down, I did what I never had done in all my life; I kneeled down and prayed to God to fulfil the promise to me, that if I called upon Him in the day of trouble, He would deliver me. After my broken and imperfect prayer was over, I drank the rum in which I had steeped the tobacco, which was so strong and rank of the tobacco that indeed I could scarce get it down. Immediately upon this I went to bed. I found presently it flew to my head violently, but I fell into a sound sleep, and waked no more till, by the sun, it must necessarily be near three o'clock in the afternoon the next day. Nay, to this hour I am partly of the opinion that I slept all the next day and night, and till almost three that day after; for otherwise I knew not how I should lose a day out of my reckoning in the days of the week, as it appeared some years after, I had done. For if I had lost it by crossing and recrossing the line, I should have lost more than one day; but, certainly, I lost a day in my account, and never knew which way.

CHAPTER SEVEN

Be that, however, one way or the other, when I awaked I found myself exceedingly refreshed, and my spirits lively and cheerful; when I got up I was stronger than I was the day before, and my stomach better, for I was hungry; and, in short, I had no fit the next day, but continued much altered for the better. This was the 29th.

The 30th was my well-day, of course, and I went abroad with my gun, but did not care to travel too far. I killed a seafowl or two, something like a goose, and brought them home, but was not very forward to eat them; so I ate some more of the turtle's eggs, which were very good. This evening I renewed the medicine which I had supposed did me good the day before — namely, the tobacco steeped in rum; only I did not take so much as before, nor did I chew any of the leaf, or hold my head over the smoke. However, I was not so well the next day, which was the 1st of July, as I hoped I should have been; for I had a little spice of the cold fit, but it was not much.

July 2. I renewed the medicine all the three ways, and dosed myself with it as at first; and doubled the quantity which I drank.

July 3. I missed the fit for good and all, though I did not recover my full strength for some weeks after. While I was thus gathering strength my thoughts ran exceedingly upon this scripture, "I will deliver thee"; and the impossibility of my deliverance lay much upon my mind in bar of my ever expecting it. But as I was discouraging myself with such thoughts it occurred to my mind that I pored so much upon my deliverance from the main affliction that I disregarded the deliverance I had received; and I was, as it were, made to ask myself such questions as these — namely, Have I not been delivered, and wonderfuly too, from sickness, from the most distressed condition that could be, and that was so frightful to me? And what notice I had taken of it: Had I done my part? God had delivered me, but I had not glorified Him; that is to say, I had not owned and been thankful for that as a deliverance. And how could I expect greater deliverance?

This touched my heart very much, and immediately I kneeled down and gave God thanks aloud for my recovery from my sickness.

July 4. In the morning I took the Bible, and, beginning at the New Testament, I began seriously to read it, and imposed upon myself to read a while every morning and every night, not tying myself to the number of chapters, but as long as my thoughts should engage me.

But leaving this part, I return to my journal.

From the 4th of July to the 14th I was chiefly employed in walking about with my gun in my hand, a little and a little at a time, as a man that was gathering up his strength after a fit of sickness; for it is hardly to be imagined how low I was, and to what weakness I was reduced.

I had been now in this unhappy island above ten months; all possibility of deliverance from this condition seemed to be entirely taken from me, and I firmly believed that no human shape had ever set foot upon that place. Having now secured my habitation, as I thought, fully to my mind, I had a great desire to make a more perfect discovery of the island, and to see what other productions I might find which I yet knew nothing of.

It was on 15th July that I began to take more particular survey of the island itself. I went up the creek first, where, as I hinted, I brought my rafts on shore. I found, after I came about two miles up that the tide did not flow any higher, and that it was no more than a little brook of running water, and very fresh and good; but this being the dry season, there was hardly any water in some parts of it, at least not enough to run in any stream so as it could be perceived. On the bank of this brook I found many pleasant savannas, or meadows, plain, smooth, and covered with grass; and on the rising parts of them, next to the higher grounds, where the water, as it might be supposed, never overflowed, I found a great deal of tobacco, green, and growing to a great and very strong stalk. There were divers other plants which I had no notion of, or understanding about, and might perhaps have virtues of their own, which I could not find out.

The next day, the 15th, I went up the same way again, and after going something farther than I had gone the day before, I found the brook, and the savannas began to cease, and the country became more woody than before. In this part I found different fruits, and, particularly, I found melons upon the ground in great abundance, and grapes upon the trees; the vines had spread indeed over the trees, and the clusters of grapes were just now in their prime, very ripe and rich. I found an excellent use for these grapes, and that was to cure or dry them in the sun, and keep them as dried grapes or raisins are kept; which I thought would be, as indeed they were, as wholesome as agreeable to eat, when no grapes might be to be had.

I spent all that evening there, and went not back to my habitation, which, by the way, was the first night, as I might say, I had lain from home. In the night I took my first contrivance, and got up into a tree, where I slept well; and the next morning proceeded upon my discovery, travelling near four miles, as I might judge by the length of the valley, keeping still due north, with a range of hills on the south and north side of me.

At the end of this march I came to an opening, where the country seemed to descend to the west, and a little spring of fresh water, which issued out of the side of the hill by me, ran the other way, that is due east; and the country appeared so fresh, so green, so flourishing, everything being in a constant verdure, of flourish of spring, that it looked like a planted garden.

I descended a little on the side of that delicious vale, surveying it with a secret kind of leasure (though mixed with my other afflicting thoughts) — to think that this was all my own, that I was king and lord of all this country indefeasibly, and had a right of possession; and if I could convey it, I might have it in inheritance, as completely as any lord of a manor in England. I saw here abundance of cocotrees, orange, and lemon, and citron trees, but all wild, and very few bearing any fruit, at least not then. However, the green limes that I gathered were not only pleasant to eat, but very wholesome; and I mixed their juice afterwards with water, which made it very wholesome, and very cool, and refreshing.

I found now I had business enough to gather and carry home; and I resolved to lay up a store, as well of grapes as limes and lemons, to furnish myself for the wet season, which I knew was approaching.

In order to this, I gathered a great heap of grapes in one place and a lesser heap in another place, and a great parcel of limes and lemons in another place; and, taking a few of each with me, I travelled homeward, and resolved to come again, and bring a bag or sack, or what I could make to carry the rest home.

Accordingly, having spent three days in this journey, I came home; — so I must now call my tent and my cave. But, before I got thither the grapes were spoiled — the richness of the fruits and the weight of the juice having broken them, and bruised them, they were good for little or nothing; as to the limes, they were good, but I could bring but a few.

The next day, being the 19th, I went back, having made me two small bags to bring home my harvest. But I was surprised when, coming to my heap of grapes, which were so rich when I gathered them, I found them all spread about, trod to pieces, and dragged about, some here, some there, and abundance eaten and devoured. By this I concluded there were some wild creatures thereabouts which had done this, but what they were I knew not.

However, as I found that there was no laying them up on heaps, and no carrying them away in a sack, but that one way they would be crushed with their own weight, and the other way they would be destroyed, I took another course; for I gathered a large quantity of the grapes, and hung them up upon the out branches for the trees, that they might cure and dry in the sun; and as for the limes and lemons, I carried as many back as I could well stand under.

When I came home from this journey I contemplated with great pleasure the fruitfulness of that valley and the pleasantness of the situation, the security from storms on that side the water, and the water, and the wood, and concluded that I had pitched upon a place to fix my abode which was by far the worst part of the country. Upon the whole I began to consider of removing my habitation, and to look out for a place equally safe as where I now was situate, if possible, in that pleasant fruitful part of the island.

This thought ran long in my head, and I was exceeding fond of it for some time, the pleasantness of the place tempting me; but when I came to a nearer view of it, and to consider that I was now by the seaside, where it was at least possible that something might happen to my advantage, and by the same ill fate that brought me hither might bring some other unhappy wretches to the same place: and though it was scarce possible that any such thing should ever happen, yet to enclose myself among the hills and woods, in the centre of the island, was to anticipate my bondage, and to render such an affair not only improbable but impossible; and that, therefore, I ought not by any means to remove.

However, I was so enamoured of this place, that I spent much of my time there for the whole remaining part of the month of July; and though, upon second thoughts, I resolved as above, not to remove, yet to build me a little kind of a bower, and surrounded it at a distance with a strong fence, being a double hedge, as high as I could reach, well staked, and filled between with brushwood; and here I lay very secure, sometimes two or three nights together, always going over it with a ladder as before; so that I fancied now I had my country-house and my seacoast house. And this work took me up to the beginning of August.

I had but newly-finished my fence and begun to enjoy my labour, but the rains came on, and made me stick close to my first habitation. For though I had made me a tent like the other, with a piece of sail, and spread it very well, yet I had not the shelter of a hill to keep me from storms, nor a cave behind me to retreat into when the rains were extraordinary.

About the beginning of August, as I said, I had finished my bower and began to enjoy myself. The 3rd of August I found the grapes I had hung up were perfectly dried, and, indeed, were excellent good raisins of the sun; so I began to take them down from the trees, and it was very happy that I did so, for the rains which followed would have spoiled them, and I had lost the best part of my winter food, for I had above two hundred large bunches of them. No sooner had I taken them all down, and carried most of them home to my cave, but it began to rain, and from hence, which was the 14th of August, it rained more or less every day till the middle of October; and sometimes so violently that I could not stir out of my cave for several days.

From the 14th of August to the 26th incessant rain, so that I couldn't stir, and was now very careful not to be much wet. In this confinement I began to be straitened for food, but venturing out twice, I one day killed a goat, and the last day, which was the 26th, found a very large tortoise, which was a treat to me; and my food was regulated thus; — I ate a bunch of raisins for my breakfast, a piece of the goat's flesh or of the turtle for my dinner broiled — for to my great misfortune I had no vessel to boil or stew anything — and two or three of the turtle's eggs for my supper.

During this confinement in my cover by the rain I worked daily two or three hours at enlarging my cave, and by degrees worked it on towards one side till I came to the outside of the hills, and made a door, or way out, which came beyond my fence or wall, and so I came in and out this way. But I was not perfectly easy at lying so open; for as I had managed myself before, I was in a perfect enclosure, whereas now I thought I lay exposed and open for anything to come in upon me. And yet I could not perceive that there was any living thing to fear, the biggest creature that I had yet seen upon the island being a goat.

September 30th. I was now come to the unhappy anniversary of my landing. I cast up the notches on my post, and found I had been on shore 365 days. I kept this day as a solemn fast, setting it apart to religious exercise, prostrating myself on the ground with the most serious humiliation, confessing my sins to God, acknowledging His righteous judgements upon me, and praying to Him to have mercy on me through Jesus Christ. And having not tasted the last refreshment for twelve hours, even till the going down of the sun, I then ate a biscuit-cake and a bunch of grapes and went to bed, finishing the day as I began it.

I had all this time observed no Sabbath-day; for as at first I had no sense of religion upon my mind, I had after some time omitted to distinguish the weeks by making a longer notch than ordinary for the Sabbath-day, and so did not really know what any of the days were. But now, having cast up the days as above, I found I had been there a year, so I divided it into weeks, and set apart every seventh day for Sabbath; though I found at the end of my account I had lost a day or two in my reckoning.

A little after this my ink began to fail me, and so I contented myself to use it more sparingly, and to write down only the most remarkable events of my life, without continuing a daily memorandum of other things.

The rainy season and the dry season began now to appear regularly to me; and I learned to divide them, so as to provide for them accordingly. But I bought all my experience before I had it; and this I am going to relate was one of the most discouraging experiments that I made at all. I have mentioned that I had saved the few ears of barley and rice which I had so surprisingly found springing up, as I thought of themselves, and believe there were about thirty stalks of rice, and about twenty of barley. And now I thought it a proper time to sow it after the rains, the sun being in its southern position going from me.

Accordingly I dug up a piece of ground as well as I could with my wooden spade, and dividing it into two parts, I sowed my grain; but as I was sowing it casually occurred to my thoughts that I would not sow it all at first, because I did not know when was the proper time for it, so I sowed about two-thirds of the seed, leaving about a handful of each.

It was a great comfort to me afterwards that I did so, for not one grain of that I sowed this time came to anything; for the dry months following, the earth having had no rain after the seed was sown, it had no moisture to assist its growth, and never came up at all till the wet season had come again, and then it grew as if it had been but newly-sown.

Finding my first seed did not grow, which I easily imagined was by the drought, I sought for a moister piece of ground near my new bower, and sowed the rest of my seed in February, a little before the vernal equinox; and this having the rainy months of March and April to water it, sprung up very pleasantly, and yielded a very good crop. But having part of the seed left only and not daring to sow all that I had, I had but a small quantity at last, my whole crop not amounting to above half a peck of each kind.

But by this experiment I was made master of my business, and knew exactly when the proper season was to sow; and that I might expect two seedtimes and two harvests each year.

While this corn was growing I made a little discovery, which was of use to me afterwards. As soon as the rains were over and the weather began to settle, which was about the month of November, I made a visit up the country to my bower, where, though I had not been some months, yet I found all things just as I left them. The circle, or double hedge, that I had made was not only firm and entire, but the stakes, which I had cut out of some trees that grew thereabouts, were all shot out and grown with long branches as much as a willow-tree usually shoots the first year after lopping its head. I could not tell what tree to call it that these stakes were cut from. I was surprised and yet very well pleased to see the young trees grow; and I pruned them, and led them up to grow as much alike as I could; and it is scarce credible how beautiful a figure they grew into in three years. So that, though the hedge made a circle of about twenty-five yards in diameter, yet the trees (for such I might now call them) soon covered it; and it was a complete shade, sufficient to lodge under all the dry season.

This made me resolve to cut some more stakes, and make me a hedge like this in a semicircle round my wall — I mean that of my first dwelling — which I did; and placing the trees or stakes in a double row, at about eight yards distance from my first fence, they grew presently, and were at first a fine cover to my habitation, and afterwards served for a defence also, as I shall observe in its order.

CHAPTER EIGHT

In this time I found much employment (and very suitable also to the time), for I found great occasion of many things which I had no way to furnish myself with but by hard labour and constant application; particularly I tried many ways to make myself a basket, but all twigs I could get for the purpose proved so brittle that they would do nothing.

Accordingly the next day I went to my country house, as I called it, and cutting some of the smaller twigs, I found them to my purpose as much as I could desire; whereupon I came the next time prepared with a hatchet to cut down a quantity, which I soon found, for there was great plenty of them. These I set up to dry within my circle or hedge, and when they were fit for use I carried them to my cave, and here during the next season, I employed myself in making, as well as I could, a great number of baskets, both to carry earth, or to carry or lay up anything as I had occasion; and though I did not finish them very handsomely, yet I made them sufficiently serviceable for my purpose; and thus afterwards I took care never to be without them. And as my wickerware decayed I made more; especially I made strong deep baskets to place my corn in instead of sacks, when I should come to have any quantity of it.

I mentioned before that I had a great mind to see the whole island, and that I had travelled up the brook, and so on to where I built my bower, and where I had an opening quite to the sea on the other side of the island. I now resolved to travel quite across the country to the seashore on that side; so taking my gun, a hatchet, and my dog, and a larger quantity of powder and shot than usual, with two biscuit-cakes, and a great bunch of raisins in my pouch for my store, I began my journey. When I had passed the vale where my bower stood as above, I came within view of the sea to the west, and it being a very clear day I fairly descried land, whether an island or a continent I could not tell; but it lay very high, extending from the west to the west-south-west at a very great distance. By my guess it could not be less than fifteen or twenty leagues off.

I could not tell what part of the world this might be, otherwise than that I knew it must be part of America, and, as I concluded by all my observations, must be near the Spanish dominions; and perhaps was all inhabited by savages, where if I should have landed, I had been in a worse condition that I was now.

With these considerations I walked very leisurely forward. I found that side of the island where I now was much pleasanter than mine; the open or savanna fields sweet, adorned with flowers and grass, and full of very fine woods. I saw abundance of parrots, and fain I would have caught one, if possible. to have kept it to be tame, and taught it to speak to me. I did, after some painstaking, catch a young parrot, for I knocked it down with a stick, and having recovered it I brought it hime; but it was some years before I could make him speak. However, at last I taught him to call me by my name very familiarly. But the accident that followed, though it be a trifle, will be very diverting in its place.

I was exceedingly diverted with this journey. I found in the low grounds hares, as I thought them to be, and foxes; but they differed greatly from all the other kinds I had met with, nor could I satisfy myself to eat them, though I killed several. But I had no need to be venturous, for I had no want of food, and of that which was very good too; especially these three sorts — namely, goats, pigeons, and turtle or tortoise, which, added to my grapes, Leadenhall Market could not have furnished a table better than I in proportion to the company.

As soon as I came to the sea-shore I was surprised to see that I had taken up my lot on the worst side of the island; for here, indeed, the shore was covered with innumerable turtles, whereas on the other side which I had found but three in a year and a half. Here was also an infinite number of fowls of many kinds; some which I had seen, and some which I had not seen of before — and many of them very good meat — but such as I knew not the names of, except those called penguins.

I could have shot as many as I pleased, but was very sparing of my powder and shot, and therefore had more mind to kill a she-goat if I could, which I could better feed on; and though there were many goats here — more than on my side of the island — yet it was with much more difficulty that I could come near them, the country being flat and even, and they saw me much sooner than when I was on the hill.

I confess this side of the country was much pleasanter than mine; but yet I had not the least inclination to remove, for as I was fixed in my habitation, it became natural to me, and I seemed all the while I was here to be as it were upon a journey, and from home. However, I travelled along the shore of the sea towards the east, I suppose about twelve miles; and then, setting up a great pole upon the shore for a mark, I concluded I would go home again, and that the next journey I took should be on the other side of the island east from my dwelling, and so round till I came to my post again; of which in its place.

I took another way to come back than that I went, thinking I could easily keep all the island so much in my view that I could not miss finding my first dwelling by viewing the country. But I found myself mistaken; for being come about two or three miles, I found myself descended into a very large valley, but so surrounded with hills, and those hills covered with wood, that I could not see which was my way by any direction but that of the sun, nor even then, unless I knew very well the position of the sun at that time of the day.

It happened, to my further misfortune, that the weather proved hazy for three or four days while I was in this valley; and not being able to see the sun, I wandered about very uncomfortably, and at last was obliged to find out the seaside, look for my post, and come back the same way I went. And then by easy journeys I turned homeward, the weather being exceeding hot, and my gun, ammunition, hatchet, and other things very heavy.

In this journey, my dog surprised a young kid, and seized upon it, and I running in to take hold of it, caught it, and saved it alive from the dog. I had a great mind to bring home if I could; for I had often been musing whether it might not be possible to get a kid or two, and so raise a breed of tame goats which might supply me when my powder and shot should be all spent.

I made a collar to this little creature, and with a string which I made of some rope-yarn, which I always carried about me, I led him along, though with some difficulty, till I came to my bower; and there I enclosed him and left him, for I was very impatient to be at home, from whence I had been absent above a month.

I cannot express what a satisfaction it was to me to come into my old hutch and lie down in my hammock-bed. This little wandering journey, without settled place of abode, had been so unpleasant to me, that my own house, as I called it to myself, was a perfect settlement to me compared to that; and it rendered everything about me so comfortable that I resolved I would never go a great way from it again while it should be my lot to stay on the island.

I reposed myself here a week, to rest and regale myself after my long journey; during which most of the time was taken up in the weighty affair of making a cage for my poll, who began now to be a mere domestic, and to be mighty well acquainted with me. Then I began to think of the poor kid which I had penned in within my little circle, and resolved to go and fetch it home or give it some food. Accordingly, I went, and found it where I had left it; for indeed, it could not get out, but almost starved for want of food. I went and cut boughs of trees and branches of such shrubs as I could find, and threw it over; and having fed it, I tied it as I did before, to lead it away. But it was so tame with being hungry that I had no need to have tied it, for it followed me like a dog; and as I continually fed it, the creature became so loving, so gentle, and so fond, that it became from that time one of my domestics also, and would never leave me afterwards.

The rainy season of the autumnal equinox was now come, and I kept the 30th of September in the same solemn manner as before; being the anniversary of my landing on the island, having now been there two years, and no more prospect of being delivered than the first day I came there. I spent the whole day in humble and thankful acknowledgments of the many wonderful mercies which my solitary condition was attended with, and without which it might have been infinitely more miserable.

With patience and labour I went through many things and, indeed, everything that my circumstances made necessary to me to do, as will appear by what follows. I was now — in the months of November and December — expecting my crop of barley and rice. The ground I had manured or dug up for them was not great; for, as I observed, my seed of each was not above the quantity of half a peck, for I had lost one whole crop by sowing in the dry season. But now my crop promised very well, when on a sudden I found I was in danger of losing it all again by enemies of several sorts, which it was scarce possible to keep from it; as, first, the goats and wild creatures which I called hares, who, tasting the sweetness of the blade, lay in it night and day as soon as it came up, and ate it so close that it could get no time to shoot up into stalk. This I saw no remedy for but making an enclosure about it with a hedge; which I did with a great deal of toil, and the more because it required speed. However, as my arable land was but small, suited to my crop, I got it totally well fenced in about three weeks' time; and shooting some of the creatures in the daytime, I set my dog to guard it in the night, tying him up to a stake at the gate, where he would stand and bark all night long. So in a little time the enemies forsook the place, and the corn grew very strong and well, and began to ripen apace.

But, as the beasts ruined me before while my corn was in the blade, so the birds were as likely to ruin me now when it was in the ear; for going along by the place to see how it thrived, I saw my little crop surrounded with fowls of I know not how many sorts, who stood as it were watching till I should be gone. I immediately let fly among them, for I always had my gun with me I had no sooner shot but there rose up a little cloud of fowls — which I had not seen at all — from among the corn itself.

This touched me sensibly, for I foresaw that in a few days they would devour all my hopes; that I should be starved, and never be able to raise a crop at all; and what to do I could not tell. However, I resolved not to lose my corn, if possible, though I should watch it night and day. In the first place, I went among it to see what damage was already done; and found they had spoiled a good deal of it, but that, as it was yet too green for them, the loss was not so great but that the remainder was like to be a good crop if it could be saved.

I stayed by it to load my gun; and then coming away I could easily see the thieves sitting upon all the trees about me, as if they only waited till I was gone away. And the event proved it to be so; for as I walked off as if I was gone, I was no sooner out of their sight but they dropped down one by one into the corn again. I was so provoked that I could not have patience to stay till more came on, knowing that every grain that they ate now was, as it might be said, a peck loaf to me in the consequence; but coming up to the hedge I fired again and killed three of them. This was what I wished for: so I took them up, and served them as we serve notorious thieves in England — namely, hanged them in chain for a terror to others. It is impossible to imagine almost that this should have such an effect as it had; for the fowls would not only not come at the corn, but in short, they forsook all that part of the island, and I could never see a bird near the place as long as my scarecrows hung there.

This I was very glad of, you may be sure; and about the latter end of December, which was our second harvest of the year, I reaped my crop. I was sadly put to it for a scythe or a sickle to cut it down; and all I could do was to make one as well as I could out of one of the broad swords or cutlasses which I saved among the arms out of the ship. However, as my first crop was but small, I had no great difficulty to cut it down. In short, I reaped it my way, for I cut off nothing but the ears, and carried it away in a great basket which I had made, and so rubbed it out with my hands; and at the end of all my harvesting I found that out of my half-peck of seed I had near two bushels of rice and above two bushels and a half of barley — that is to say, by my guess, for I had no measure at that time.

CHAPTER NINE

I foresaw that in time it would please God to supply me with bread. And yet here I was perplexed again: for I neither knew how to grind or make meal of my corn, or, indeed, how to clean it and part it; nor, if made into meal, how to make bread of it; and if how to make it, yet I knew not how to bake it. These things being added to my desire of having a good quantity of store, and to secure a constant supply, I resolved not to taste any of this crop, but to preserve it all for seed against the next season; and in the meantime to employ all my study and hours of working to accomplish this great work of providing myself with corn bread.

First, I had no plough to turn up the earth, no spade or shovel to dig it. Well, this I conquered by making a wooden spade, as I observed before. But this did my work in but a wooden manner; and though it cost me a great many days to make it, yet for want of iron it not only wore out the sooner, but made my work the harder, and made it be performed much worse. However, this I bore with, and was content to work it out with patience, and bear with the badness of the performance. When the corn was sowed I had no harrow, but was forced to go over it myself, and drag a great heavy bough of a tree over it, to scratch it, as it may be called, rather than rake or harrow it.

When it was growing and grown, I have observed already, how many things I wanted, to fence secure it, mow or reap it, cure and carry it home, thrash, part it from the chaff, and save it. Then I wanted a mill to grind it, sieves to dress it, yeast and salt to make it into bread, and an oven to bake it; and yet all these things I did without, as shall be observed; and yet the corn was an inestimable comfort and advantage to me too. All this, as I said, made everything laborious and tedious to me, but that there was no help for, neither was my time so much loss to me, because, as I had divided it, a certain part of it was every day appointed to these works. And as I resolved to use none of the corn for bread till I had a greater quantity by me, I had the next six months to apply myself wholly by labour and invention to furnish myself with utensils proper for the performing all the operations necessary for the making the corn (when I had it) fit for my use.

But, first, I was to prepare more land, for I had now seed enough to sow above an acre of ground. Before I did this I had a week's work at least to make me a spade; which, when it was done, was but a sorry one indeed, and very heavy, and required double labour to work with it. However, I went through that, and sowed my seed in two large flat pieces of ground as near my house as I could find them to my mind, and fenced them in with a good hedge, the stakes of which were all cut of that wood which I had set before, and knew it would grow; so that in one year's time I knew should have a quick or living hedge, that would want but little repair. This work was not so little as to take me up less than three months, because great part of that time was of the wet season, when I could not go abroad.

Within doors — that is, when it rained, and I could not go out — I found employment on the following occasions, always observing that all the while I was at work I diverted myself with talking to my parrot, and teaching him to speak; and I quickly learned him to know his own name and at last to speak it out pretty loud — POLL, which was the first word I ever heard spoken in the island by any mouth but my own. This, therefore, was not my work, but an assistant to my work; for now, as I said, I had a great employment upon my hands, as follows — namely, I had long studied by some means or other to make myself some earthen vessels, which indeed I wanted sorely, but knew not where to come at them. However, considering the heat of the climate, I did not doubt but if I could find out any such clay, I might botch up some such pot as might, being dried in the sun, be hard enough and strong enough to bear handling, and to hold anything that was dry and required to be kept so. And as this was necessary in the preparing corn, meal, which was the thing I was upon, I resolved to make some as large as I could, and fit only to stand like jars to hold what should be put into them.

It would make the reader pity me, or rather laugh at me, to tell how many awkward ways I took to raise this paste; what odd, misshapen, ugly things I made; how many of them fell in, and how many fell out, the clay not being stiff enough to bear its own weight; how many cracked by the over-violent heat of the sun, being set out too hastily; and how many fell in pieces with only removing as well before as after they were dried; and, in a word, how after having laboured hard to find the clay, to dig it, to temper it, to bring it home and work it, I could not make above two large earthen ugly things — I cannot call them jars — in about two months' labour.

However, as the sun baked these two very dry and hard, I lifted them very gently up, and set them down again in two great wicker baskets which I had made on purpose for them, that they might not break; and as between the pot and the basket there was a little room to spare, I stuffed it full of rice and barley straw. And these two pots being to stand always dry, I thought would hold my dry corn, and perhaps the meal, when the corn was bruised.

Though I miscarried so much in my design for large pots, yet I made several smaller things with better success — such as little round pots, flat dishes, pitchers, and pipkins, and any thing my hand turned to; and the heat of the sun baked them strangely hard.

But all this would not answer my end, which was to get an earthen pot to hold what was liquid, and bear the fire, which none of these could do. It happened after some time, making a pretty large fire for cooking my meat, when I went to put it out after I had done with it, I found a broken piece of one of my earthenware vessels in the fire burned as hard as a stone, and red as a tile. I was agreeably surprised to see it, and said to myself that certainly they might be made to burn whole if they would burn broken.

This set me to studying how to order my fire, so as to make it burn me some pots. I had no notion of a kiln, such as the potters burn in; or of glazing them with lead, though I had some lead to do it with; but I placed three large pipkins and two or three pots in a pile, one upon another, and placed my firewood all round it, with a heap of embers under them. I piled the fire with fresh fuel round the outside and upon the top, till I saw the pots in the inside red hot quite through, and observed that they did not crack at all. When I saw them clear red, I let them stand in that heat about five or six hours, till I found one of them, though it did not crack, did melt or run; for the sand which was mixed with the clay melted by the violence of the heat, and would have run into glass if I had gone on, so I slacked my fire gradually, till the pots began to abate of the red colour; and watching them all night that I might not let the fire abate too fast, in the morning I had three very good — I will not say handsome — pipkins and two other earthen pots as hard burned as could be desired, and one of them perfectly glazed with the running of the sand.

No joy at a thing of so mean a nature was ever equal to mine when I found I had made an earthen pot that would bear the fire; and I had hardly patience to stay till they were cold before I set one upon the fire again with some water in it to boil me some meat, which it did admirably well. And with a piece of a kid I made some very good broth, though I wanted oatmeal, and several other ingredients requisite to make it so good as I would have had it been.

My next concern was, to get me a stone mortar to stamp or beat some corn in; for as to the mill, there was no thought at arriving to that perfection of art with one pair of hands. To supply this want I was at a great loss; for of all trades in the world, I was as perfectly unqualified for a stone-cutter as for any whatever; neither had I any tools to go about it with. I spent many a day to find out a great stone big enough to cut hollow, and make fit for a mortar, and could find none at all, except what was in the solid rock, and which I had no way to dig or cut out; nor indeed, were the rocks in the island of hardness sufficient, but were all of a sandy crumbling stone, which neither would bear the weight of a heavy pestle, or would break the corn without filling it with sand. So after a great deal of time lost in searching for a stone, I gave it over, and resolved to look out for a great block of hard wood, which I found indeed much easier; and getting one as big as I had strength to stir, I rounded it, and formed it in the outside with my axe and hatchet, and then, with the help of fire and infinite labour, made a hollow place in it, as the Indians in Brazil make their canoes. After this I made a great heavy pestle or beater of the wood called the iron-wood, and this I prepared and laid by against I had my next crop of corn, when I proposed to myself to grind, or rather pound, my corn into meal to make my bread.

My next difficulty was to make a sieve, or search, to dress my meal, and to part it from the bran and the husk, without which I did not see it possible I could have any bread. This was a most difficult thing so much as but to think on; for to be sure I had nothing like the necessary thing to make it — I mean fine thin canvas, or stuff to search the meal through. And here I was at a full stop for many months; nor did I really know what to do. Linen I had none left, but what was mere rags. I had goats' hair but neither knew how to weave it or spin it; and had I known how, there were no tools to work it with. All the remedy that I found for this was, that at last I did remember I had among the seamen's clothes which were saved out of the ship some neckcloths of calico or muslin; and with some pieces of these I made three small sieves, but proper enough for the work. And thus I made shift for some years. How I did afterwards I shall show in its place.

The baking part was the next thing to be considered, and how I should make bread when I came to have corn; for first, I had no yeast. As to that part, as there was no supplying the want, so I did not concern myself much about it; but for an oven I was indeed in great pain. At length I found out an experiment for that also, which was this — I made some earthen vessels very broad, but not deep; that is to say, about two foot diameter, and not above nine inches deep, these I burned in the fire, as I had done the other, and laid them by; and when I wanted to bake, I made a great fire upon my hearth, which I had paved with some square tiles of my own making and burning also — but I should not call them square.

When the firewood was burned pretty much, into embers, or live coals, I drew forward upon this hearth, so as to cover it all over, and there I let them lie till the earth was very hot; then sweeping away all the embers, I set down my loaf or loaves, and whelming down the earthenpot upon them, drew the embers all round the outside of the pot, to keep in and add to the heat; and thus, as well as in the best oven in the world, I baked my barley loaves, and became in a little time a mere pastrycook into the bargain; for I made myself several cakes of the rice, and puddings. Indeed I made no pies, neither had I anything to put into them supposing I had, except the flesh either of fowls or goats.

It need not be wondered at if all these things took me up most part of the third year of my abode here; for it is to be observed that, in the intervals of these things, I had my new harvest and husbandry to manage; for I reaped my corn in its season, and carried it home as well as I could, and laid it up in the ear in my large baskets till I had time to rub it out, for I had no floor to thrash it on, or instrument to thrash it with.

And now indeed my stock of corn increasing, I really wanted to build my barns bigger. I wanted a place to lay it up in, for the increase of the corn now yielded me so much that I had of the barley about twenty bushels, and of the rice as much or more; insomuch that now I resolved to begin to use it freely, for my bread had been quite gone a great while. Also I resolved to see what quantity would be sufficient for me a whole year, and to sow but once a year.

Upon the whole, I found that the forty bushels of barley and rice was much more than I could consume in a year, so I resolved to sow just the same quantity every year that I sowed the last, in hopes that such a quantity every year would fully provide me with bread, &c.

All the while these things were doing you may be sure my thoughts ran many times upon the prospect of land which I had seen from the other side of the island; and I was not without secret wishes that I were on shore there, fancying the seeing the mainland, and thinking that in an inhabited country I might find some way or other to convey myself farther, and perhaps at last find some means of escape.

But all this while I made no allowance for the dangers of such a condition, and how I might fall into the hands of savages, and perhaps such as I might have reason to think far worse than the lions and tigers of Africa. That if I once came into their power I should run a hazard more than a thousand to one of being killed, and perhaps of being eaten; for I had heard that the people of the Caribbean coasts were cannibals, or man-eaters; and I knew by the latitude that I could not be far off from that shore.

Then I thought I would go and look at our ship's boat, which, as I have said, was blown up upon the shore a great way in the storm when we were first cast away. She lay almost where she did at first, but not quite; and was turned by the force of the waves and the winds almost bottom upward against a high ridge of beachy rough sand, but no water about her as before.

If I had had hands to have refitted her, and to have launched her into the water the boat would have done well enough, and I might have gone back into the Brazils with her easily enough; but I might have foreseen that I could no more turn her and set her upright upon her bottom than I could remove the island. However, I went to the woods and cut levers and rollers and brought them to the boat, resolved to try what I could do, suggesting to myself that if I could but turn her down, I might easily repair the damage she had received, and she would be a very good boat, and I might go to sea in her very easily.

I spared no pains indeed in this piece of fruitless toil, and spent, I think three of four weeks about it. At last, finding it impossible to heave it up with my little strength, I fell to digging away the sand to undermine it, and so to make it fall down, setting pieces of wood to thrust and guide it right in the fall.

But when I had done this I was unable to stir it up again or to get under it, much less to move it forward towards the water, so I was forced to give it over; and yet, though I gave over the hopes of the boat, my desire to venture over for the main increased rather than decreased as the means for it seemed impossible.

This at length put me upon thinking whether it was not possible to make myself a canoe, such as the natives of those climates make, even without tools, or, as I might say, without hands — namely, of the trunk of a great tree.

I went to work upon this boat the most like a fool that ever man did who had any of his senses awake. I pleased myself with the design, without determining whether I was ever able to undertake it; not but that difficulty of launching my boat came often into my head, but I put a stop to my own enquiries into it, by this foolish answer which I gave myself, "Let's first make it; I'll warrant I'll find some way or other to get it along when 'tis done."

I felled a cedar-tree — I question much whether Solomon ever had such a one for a building of the temple at Jerusalem! It was five feet ten inches diameter at the lower part next the stump, and four feet eleven inches diameter at the end of twenty-two feet after which it lessened for a while and parted into branches. It was not without infinite labour that I felled this tree. I was twenty days hacking and hewing at it at the bottom. I was fourteen more getting the branches and limbs and the vast spreading head of it cut off, which I hacked and hewed through with axe and hatchet and inexpressible labour. After this it cost me a month to shape it and dub it to a proportion, and to something like the bottom of a boat, that it might swim upright as it ought to do. It cost me near three months more to clear the inside, and work it out so as to make an exact boat of it. This I did indeed without fire, by mere mallet and chisel, and by the dint of hard labour.

But all my devices to get it into the water failed me, though they cost me infinite labour too. It lay about one hundred yards from the water, and not more; but the first inconvenience was, it was up-hill towards the creek. Well, to take away this discouragement, I resolved to dig into the surface of the earth, and to make a declivity. This I began, and it cost me a prodigious deal of pains; — but who grudge pains that have their deliverance in view? But when this was worked through, and this difficulty managed, it was still much at one; for I could no more stir the canoe than I could the other boat.

Then I measured the distance of ground, and resolved to cut a dock or canal to bring the water up to the canoe, seeing I could not bring the canoe down to the water. Well, I begin this work, and when I began to enter into it, and calculate how deep it was to be dug, how broad, how the stuff to be thrown out, I found that, by the number of hands I had, being none but my own, it must have been ten or twelve years before I should have gone through with it; for the shore lay high, so that at the upper end it must have been at least twenty foot deep. So at length, though with great reluctancy, I gave this attempt over also.

This grieved me heartily; and now I saw, though too late, the folly of beginning a work before we count the cost, and before we judge rightly of our own strength to go through with it.

In the middle of this work I finished my fourth year in this place, and kept my anniversary with the same devotion, and with as much comfort as ever before; for by a constant study and serious application of the Word of God, and by the assistance of His Grace, I gained a different knowledge from what I had before.

CHAPTER TEN

I had now been here so long that many things which I brought on shore for my help were either quite gone or very much wasted and near spent.

My ink, as I observed, had been gone for some time, all but a very little, which I eked out with water till it was so pale it scarce left any appearance of black upon the paper. As long as it lasted made one that answered indifferently well. The main difficulty I found was to make it to let down. I could make it to spread, but if it did not let down too and draw in, it was not portable for me any way but just over my head, which would not do. However, at last, as I said, I made one to answer, and covered it with skins, the hair upwards, so that it cast off the rains like a penthouse, and kept off the sun so effectually that I could walk out in the hottest of the weather with greater advantage than I could before in the coolest; and when I had no need of it, could close it and carry it under my arm.

I cannot say that after this, for five years, any extraordinary thing happened to me, but I lived on in the same course, in the same posture and place, just as before. The chief things I was employed in, besides my yearly labour of planting my barley and rice and curing my raisins, of both which I always kept up just enough to have sufficient stock of one year's provisions beforehand; I say, besides this yearly labour and my daily labour of going out with my gun, I had one labour to make me a canoe, which at last I finished; so that, by digging a canal to it of six feet wide and four feet deep, I brought it into the creek, almost half a mile.

However, though my little periagua was finished, yet the size of it was not at all answerable to the design which I had in view when I made the first — I mean, of venturing over to the terra firma, where it was above forty miles broad. Accordingly, the smallness of my boat assisted to put an end to that design, and now I thought no more of it. But as I had a boat, my next design was to make a tour round the island; for as I had been on the other side in one place, crossing, as I have

I made use of it to minute down the days of the month on which any remarkable thing happened to me, and first by casting up times past. I remember that there was a strange occurrence of days in the various providences which befell me, and which, if I had been superstitiously inclined to observe days as fatal or fortunate, I might have had reason to have looked upon with a great deal of curiosity.

First, I had observed that the same day that I broke away from my father and my friends, and ran away to Hull, in order to go to sea, the same day afterwards I was taken by the Sallee man-of-war, and made a slave.

The same day of the year that I escaped out of the wreck of that ship in Yarmouth Roads, that same day — years afterwards — I made my escape from Sallee in the boat.

The same day of the year I was born on — namely the 30th of September — the same day I had my life so miraculously saved twenty-six years after, when I was cast on shore on this island, so that my wicked life and my solitary life began both on a day.

The next thing to my ink's being was that of my bread — I mean the biscuit which I brought out of the ship. This I had husbanded to the last degree, allowing myself but one cake of bread a day for above a year, and yet I was quite without bread for near a year before I got any corn of my own; and great reason I had to be thankful that I had any at all, the getting it being, as has been already observed, next to miraculous.

My clothes began to decay too mightily. As to linen, I had none a good while, except some checkered shirts which I found in the chests of the other seamen, and wich I carefully preserved, because many times I could bear no other clothes on but a shirt: and it was a very great help to me that I had among all the men's clothes of the ship, almost three dozen of shirts. There were also several thick watch-coats of the seamen's, which were left indeed, but they were too hot to wear. And though it is true that the weather was so violently hot that there was no need of clothes, yet I could not go quite naked: not though I had been inclined to it, which I was not, nor could not abide the thoughts of it, though I was all alone.

The reason why I could not go quite naked was, I could not bear the heat of the sun so well when quite naked as with some clothes on; nay, the very heat frequently blistered my skin, whereas, with a shirt on, the air itself made some motion, and whistling under that shirt, was twofold cooler than without it. No more could I ever bring myself to go out in the heat of the sun without a cap or a hat, the heat of the sun beating with such violence as it does in that place would give me the headache presently, by darting so directly on my head without a cap or hat on, so that I could not bear it, whereas, if I put on my hat, it would presently go away.

Upon those views I began to consider about putting the few rags I had, which I called clothes, into some order. I had worn out all the waistcoats I had, and my business was now to try if I could not make jackets out of the great watch-coats which I had by me, and with such other materials as I had; so I set to work a-tailoring, or rather indeed a-botching, for I made most piteous work of it. However, I made shift to make two or three new waistcoats,

which I hoped would serve me a great while. As for breeches or drawers, I made but a very sorry shift indeed till afterward.

I saved the skins of all the creatures that I killed — I mean four-footed ones — and I had hung them up stretched out with sticks in the sun, by which means some of them were so dry and hard that they were fit for little, but others it seems were very useful. The first thing I made of these was a great cap for my head, with the hair on the outside to shoot off the rain; and this I performed so well, that after this I made me a suit of clothes wholly of skins — that is to say, a waistcoat and breeches open at knees, and both loose, for they were rather wanting to keep me cool than to keep me warm. I must not omit to acknowledge that they were wretchedly made; for if I was a bad carpenter, I was a worse tailor. However, they were such as I made very good shift with. And when I wa abroad, if it happened to rain, the hair of my wais coat and cap being outermost, I was kept very dr

After this I spent a great deal of time and pa to make me an umbrella. I was indeed in great v of one, and had a great mind to make one. I seen them made in the Brazils, where they are useful in the great heats which are there; felt the heats every jot as great here, and too, being nearer the equinox. Besides, a obliged to be much abroad, it was a mo thing to me, as well for the rains as the took a world of pains at it, and was a g before I could make anything likely to after I thought I had hit the way I spo three before I made one to my mind, already described it, over the land, so the discoveries I made in that little journey made me very eager to see other parts of the coast; and now I had a boat, I thought of nothing but sailing round the island.

For this purpose, that I might do everything with discretion and consideration, I fitted up a little mast to my boat, to put provisions, necessaries, and ammunition, &c., into, to be kept dry either from rain or the spray of the sea; and a little long hollow place I cut in the inside of the boat, where I could lay my gun, making a flap to hang down over it to keep it dry.

I fixed my umbrella also in a step at the stern, like a mast, to stand over my head, and keep the heat of the sun off me like an awning; and thus I every now and then took a little voyage upon the sea, but never went far out, not far from the little creek. But at last, being eager to view the circumference of my little kingdom, I resolved upon my tour, and accordingly I victualled my ship for the voyage, putting in two dozen of my loaves (cakes I should rather call them) of barley bread, an earthen pot full of parched rice — a food I ate a good deal of — a little bottle of rum, half a goat, and powder and shot for killing more, and two large watch-coats of those which, as I mentioned before, I had saved out of the seamen's chests; these I took, one to lie upon, and the other to cover me in the night.

It was the 6th of November, in the sixth year of my reign, or my captivity, which you please, that I set out on this voyage, and I found it much longer than I expected. For though the island itself was not very large, yet, when I came to the east side of it, I found a great ledge of rocks lie out above two leagues into the water, some above the sea, some under it; and beyond that a shoal of sand, lying dry half a league more. So that I was obliged to go a great way out to sea to double the point.

When first I discovered them I was going to give over my enterprise and come back again not knowing how far it might oblige me to go out to sea; and above all, doubting how I should get back again; so I came to an anchor — for I had made me a kind of an anchor with a piece of a broken grapling, which I got out of the ship.

Having secured my boat, I took my gun and went on shore, climbing up upon a hill which seemed to overlook that point where I saw the full extent of it, and resolved to venture.

In my viewing the sea from that hill where I stood I perceived a strong, and indeed a most furious current, which ran to the east, and even came close to the point. And I took the more notice of it, because I saw there might be some danger that when I came into it I might be carried out to sea by the strength of it, and not be able to make the island again. And, indeed, had I not gotten first up upon this hill, I believe it would have been so; for there was the same current on the other side the island, only that it set off at a farther distance. And I saw there was a strong eddy under the shore; so I had nothing to do but to get it out of the first current, and I should presently be in an eddy.

I lay here, however, two days, because the wind blowing pretty fresh at east-south-east, and that being just contrary to the said current, made a great breach of the sea upon the point; so that it was not safe for me to keep too close to the shore for the breach, nor to go too far off because of the stream.

The third day, in the morning, the wind having abated overnight, the sea was calm, and I ventured. But I am a warning piece again to all rash and ignorant pilots; for no sooner was I come to the point, when even I was not my boat's length from the shore, but I found myself in a great depth of water, and a current like the sluice of a mill. It carried my boat along with it with such violence that all I could do could not keep her so much as on the edge of it; but I found it hurried me farther and farther out from the eddy, which was on my left hand. There was no wind stirring to help me; and all I could do with my paddles signified nothing. And now I began to give myself over for lost; for as the current was on both sides the island, I knew in a few leagues distance they must join again and then I was irrecoverably gone. Nor did I see any possibility of avoiding it; so that I had no prospect before me but of perishing — not by the sea, for that was calm enough, but of starving for hunger. I had, indeed, found a tortoise on the shore as big almost as I could lift, and had tossed it into the boat; and I had a great jar of fresh water — that is to say, one of my earthen pots; but what was all this to being driven into the vast ocean, where, to be sure, there was no shore, no mainland or island for a thousand leagues at least!

And now I saw how easy it was for the providence of God to make the most miserable condition mankind could be in, worse. Now I looked back upon my desolate solitary island as the most pleasant place in the world, and all the happiness my heart could wish for was to be but there again.

Just as I had set my mast and sail, and the boat began to stretch away, I saw even by the clearness of the water some alteration of the current was near; for where the current was so strong, the water was foul; but perceiving the water clear, I found the current abate, and presently I found to the east, at about half a mile, a breach of the sea upon some rocks. These rocks, I found, caused the current to part again, and as the main stress of it ran away more southerly, leaving the rocks to the north-east, so the other returned by the repulse of the rocks, and made a strong eddy, which ran back again to the north-west, with a very sharp stream.

This eddy carried me about a league in my way back again directly towards the island, about two leagues more to the northward than the current which carried me away at first; so that when I came near the island, I found myself open to the northern shore of it — that is to say, the other end of the island opposite to that which I went out from.

When I had made something more than a league of way by the help of this current or eddy, I found it was spent, and served me no farther. However, I found that being between the two great currents, namely, that on the south side, which had hurried me away, and that on the north, which lay about a league on the other side: I say, between these two, in the wake of the island, I found the water at least still and running no way; and having still a breeze of wind fair for me, I kept on steering directly for the island, though not making such fresh way as I did before.

About four o'clock in the evening, being then within about a league of the island, I found the point of the rocks which occasioned this disaster stretching out, as is described before, to the southward, and casting off the current more southwardly had of course made another eddy to the north, and this I found very strong, not directly setting the way my course lay, which was due west, but almost full north. However, having a fresh gale, I stretched across this eddy slanting north-west, and in about an hour came within about a mile of the shore, where, it being smooth water, I soon got to land. When I was on shore, I fell on my knees and gave God thanks for my deliverance, resolving to lay aside all thoughts of my deliverance by my boat; and refreshed myself with such things as I had. I brought my boat close to the shore in a little cove that I had spied under some trees, and laid me down to sleep, being quite spent with labour and fatigue of the voyage.

I was now at a great loss which way to get home with my boat. I had run so much hazard, and knew too much the case, to think of attempting it by the way I went out; and what might be at the other side (I mean the west side) I knew not, nor had I any mind to run any more ventures; so I only resolved in the morning to make my way westward along the shore, and to see if there was no creek where I might lay up my frigate in safety, so as to have her again when I wanted her. In about three mile or thereabouts, coasting the shore, I came to a very good inlet·or bay about a mile over, which narrowed till it came to a very little rivulet or brook, where I found a very convenient harbour for my boat, and where she lay as if she had been in a little dock made on purpose for her. Here I put in, and having stowed my boat very safe, I went on shore to look about me and see where I was.

I soon found I had but a little passed by the place where I had been before, when I travelled on foot to that shore; so taking out nothing of my boat but my gun and my umbrella, for it was exceeding hot, I began my march. The way was comfortable enough after such a voyage as I had been upon, and I reached my old bower in the evening, where I found everything standing as I left it; for I always kept it in good order, being, as I said before, my country house.

I got over the fence, and laid me down in the shade to rest my limbs, for I was very weary, and fell asleep. But judge you, if you can, that read my story, what a surprise I must be in, when I was fell asleep. But judge you, if you can, that read my name several times, "Robin, Robin, Robin Crusoe; poor Robin Crusoe! Where are you, Robin Crusoe? Where are you? Where have you been?"

CHAPTER ELEVEN

I was so dead asleep at first, being fatigued with rowing, or paddling, as it is called, the first part of the day, and with walking the latter part, that I did not wake thoroughly; but dozing between sleeping and waking, thought I dreamed that somebody spoke to me. But as the voice continued to repeat, "Robin Crusoe, Robin Crusoe," at last I began to wake more perfectly, and was at first dreadfully frightened, and started up in the utmost consternation. But no sooner were my eyes open, but I saw my Poll sitting on the top of the hedge, and immediately knew that it was he that spoke to me; for just in such bemoaning language I had used to talk to him, and teach him; and he had learned it so perfectly, that he would sit upon my finger, and lay his bill close to my face, and cry, "Poor Robin Crusoe, where are you? Where have you been? How come you here?" and such things as I had taught him.

However, even though I knew it was the parrot, and that indeed it could be nobody else it was a good while before I could compose myself: first I was amazed how the creature got thither, and then how he should just keep about the place, and nowhere else. But as I was well satisfied it could be nobody but honest Poll, I got it over; and holding out my hand, and calling him by his name Poll, the sociable creature came to me, and sat upon my thumb, as he used to do, and continued talking to me, "Poor Robin Crusoe," and "How did I come here?" and "Where had I been?" just as if he had been overjoyed to see me again; and so I carried him home along with me.

I had now had enough of rambling to sea for some time, and had enough to do for many days to sit still and reflect upon the danger I had been in. In this government of my temper I remained near a year — lived a very sedate, retired life, as you may well suppose; and my thoughts being very much composed as to my condition, and fully comforted in resigning myself to the dispositions of Providence, I thought I lived really very happily in all things, except that of society.

I improved myself in this time in all the mechanic exercises which my necessities put me upon applying myself to, and I believe could, upon occasion, make a very good carpenter, especially considering how few tools I had.

Besides this, I arrived at an unexpected perfection in my earthenware, and contrived well enough to make them with a wheel, which I found infinitely easier and better; because I made things round and shapeable, which before were filthy things indeed to look at. But I think I was never more vain in my own performance, or more joyful for anything I found out, than for my being able to make a tobacco-pipe. And although it was a very ugly clumsy thing when it was done, and only burned red like other earthenware, yet, as it was hard and firm, and would draw the smoke, I was exceedingly comforted with it; for I had been always used to smoke, and there were pipes on the ship, but I forgot them at first, not knowing that there was tobacco in the island; and afterwards, when I searched the ship again, I could not find any pipes at all.

In my wickerware, also, I improved much, and made abundance of necessary baskets, as well as my invention showed me. Though not very handsome, yet they were such as were very handy and convenient for my laying things up in, or fetching things home in. For example, if I killed a goat abroad, I could hang it up in a tree, flay it, and dress it, and cut it in pieces, and bring it home in a basket; and the like by a turtle, — I could cut it up, take out the eggs, and a piece or two of the flesh, which was enough for me, and bring them home in a basket, and leave the rest behind me. Also large deep baskets were my receivers for my corn, which I always rubbed out as soon as it was dry, and cured, and kept it in great baskets.

I began now to perceive my powder abated considerably and this was a want which it was impossible for me to supply, and I began seriously to consider what I must do when I should have no more powder; that is to say, how I should do to kill any goat. I had, as is observed, in the third year of my being here, kept a young kid, and bred her up tame, and I was in hope of getting a he-goat, but I could not by any means bring it to pass, till my kid grew an old goat; and I could never find in my heart to kill her till she died at last of mere age.

But being now in the eleventh year of my residence, and as I have said, my ammunition growing low, I set myself to study some art to trap and snare the goats, to see whether I could not catch some of them alive, and particularly I wanted a she-goat great with young.

To this purpose I made snares to hamper them; and I do believe they were more than one taken in them; but my tackle was not good, for I had no wire, and I always found them broken, and my bait devoured.

At length I resolved to try a pit-fall. So I dug several large pits in the earth, in places where I had observed the goats used to feed; and over these pits I placed hurdles of my own making too, with a great weight upon them. And several times I put ears of barley, and dry rice, without setting the trap; and I could easily perceive that the goats had gone in and eaten up the corn, for I could see the mark of their feet. At length I set three traps in one night; and going the next morning, I found them all standing, and yet the bait eaten and gone. This was very discouraging. However, I altered my trap; and not to trouble you with particulars, going one morning to see my trap, I found in one of them a large old he-goat; and in one of the other, three kids — a male and two females.

As to the old one, I knew not what to do with him; he was so fierce I durst not go into the pit to him — that is to say, to go about to bring him away alive, which was what I wanted. I could have killed him; but that was not my business, nor would it answer my end. So I even let him out, and he ran away as if he had been frightened out of his wits. But I had forgot then what I learned afterwards — that hunger will tame a lion. If I had let him stay there three or four days without food, and then have carried him some water to drink, and then a little corn, he would have been as tame as one of the kids — for they are mighty sagacious, tractable creatures where they are well used.

However, for the present I let him go, knowing no better at that time. Then I went to the three kids; and taking them one by one, I tied them with strings together, and with some difficulty brought them all home.

It was a good while before they would feed; but throwing them some sweet corn, it tempted them, and they began to be tame. And now I found that if I expected to supply myself with goat-flesh when I had no powder or shot left, breeding some up tame was my only way; when, perhaps, I might have them about my house like a flock of sheep.

But then it presently occurred to me that I must keep the tame from the wild, or else they would always run wild when they grew up. And the only way for this was to have some enclosed piece of ground, well fenced with hedge or pale, to keep them in so effectually, that those within might not break out, or those without break in.

This was a great undertaking for one pair of hands. Yet, as I saw there was an absolute necessity for doing it, my first piece of work was to find out a proper piece of ground, namely, where there was likely to be herbage for them to eat, water for them to drink, and cover to keep them from the sun.

Those who understand such enclosures will think I had very little contrivance when I pitched upon a place very proper for all these, being a plain open piece of meadow-land or savanna (as our people call it in the western colonies), which had two or three little rills of fresh water in it, and at one end was very woody. I say they will smile at my forecast, when I shall tell them I began my enclosing of this piece of ground in such a manner that my hedge or pale must have been at least two mile about! Nor was the madness of it so great as to the compass, for if it was ten mile about, I was like to have time enough to do it in. But I did not consider that my goats would be as wild in so much compass as if they had had the whole island, and I should have so much room to chase them in that I should never catch them.

My hedge was begun and carried on, I believe about fifty yards, when this thought occurred to me. So I presently stopped short, and for the first beginning I resolved to enclose a piece of about one hundred and fifty yards in length, and one hundred yards in breadth; which, as it would maintain as many as I should have in any reasonable time, so, as my flock increased, I could add more ground to my enclosure.

This was acting with some prudence, and I went to work with courage. I was about three months hedging in the first piece; and till I had done it, I tethered the three kids in the best part of it, and used them to feed as near me as possible, to make them familiar; and very often I would go and carry them some ears of barley, or a handful of rice, and feed them out of my hand; so that, after my enclosure was finished, and I let them loose, they would follow me up and down, bleating after me for a handful of corn.

This answered my end. And in about a year and a half I had a flock of about three-and-forty — besides several that I took and killed for my food. And after that, I enclosed five several pieces of ground to feed them in, with little pens to drive them into, to take them as I wanted, and gates out of one piece of ground into another.

But this is not all; for now I not only had goat's flesh to feed on when I pleased, but milk too — a thing which, indeed, in my beginning, I did not so much as think of, and which, when it came into my thoughts, was really an agreeable surprise. For now I set up my dairy, and had sometimes a gallon or two of milk in a day. And as Nature, who gives supplies of food to every creature dictates even naturally how to make use of it; so I, that had never milked a cow, much less a goat, or seen butter or cheese made, very readily and handily, though after a great many essays and miscarriages, made me both butter and cheese at last.

You are to understand that now I had, as I may call it, two plantations in the island: one my little fortification or tent, with the wall about it under the rock, with the cave behind me, which by this time I had enlarged into several apartments, or caves, one within another. One of these, which was the driest and largest, and had a door out beyond my wall or fortification — that is to say beyond where my wall joined to the rock — was all filled up with the large earthen pots of which I have given an account, and with fourteen or fifteen great baskets, which would hold five or six bushels each, where I laid up my stores of provision, especially my corn, some in the ear cut off short from the straw, and the other rubbed out with my hand.

As for my wall, made, as before, with long stakes or piles, those piles grew all like trees, and were by this time grown so big, and spread so very much, that there was not the least appearance to any one's view of any habitation behind them.

Near this dwelling of mine, but a little farther within the land, and upon lower ground, lay my two pieces of cornground, which I kept duly cultivated and sowed, and which duly yielded me their harvest in its reason; and whenever I had occasion for more corn, I had more land adjoining as fit as that.

Besides this I had my country seat, and I had now a tolerable plantation there also: for first, I had my little bower, as I called it, which I kept in repair — that is to say, I kept the hedge which circled it in, constantly fitted up to its usual height, the ladder standing always in the inside. I kept the trees, which at first were no more than my stakes, but were now grown very firm and tall — I kept them always so cut that they might spread and grow thick and wild, and make the more agreeable shade, which they did effectually to my mind. In the middle of this, I had my tent always standing, being a piece of a sail spread over poles set up for that purpose, and which never wanted any repair or renewing; and under this I had made me a squab or couch, with the skins of the creatures I had killed, and with other soft things, and a blanket laid on them; such as belonged to our sea-bedding, which I had saved, and a great watch-coat to cover me; and here, whenever I had occasion to be absent from my chief seat, I took my country habitation.

Adjoining to this I had my enclosures for my cattle, that is to say, my goats; and as I had taken an inconceivable deal of pains to fence and enclose this ground, so I was so uneasy to see it kept entire, lest the goats should break through, that I never left off till with infinite labour I had stuck the outside of the hedge so full of small stakes, and so near to one another, that it was rather a pale than a hedge, and there was scarce room to put a hand through between them; which, afterwards, when these stakes grew, as they all did in the next rainy season, made the enclosure strong like a wall; indeed, stronger than any wall.

In this place, also, I had my grapes growing, which I principally depended on for my winter store of raisins; and which I never failed to preserve very carefully, as the best and most agreeable dainty of my whole diet; and, indeed, they were not agreeable only, but physical, wholesome, nourishing, and refreshing to the last degree.

As this was also about halfway between the other habitation and the place where I had laid up my boat, I generally stayed and lay here in my way thither; for I used frequently to visit my boat, and I kept all things about or belonging to her in very good order. Sometimes I went out in her to divert myself; but no more hazardous voyages would I go, nor scarce ever above a stone's throw or two from the shore, I was so apprehensive of being hurried out of my knowledge again by the currents, or, winds, or any other accident. But now I come to a new scene of life.

It happened one day about noon, going towards my boat, I was exceedingly surprised with the print of a man's naked foot on the shore, which was very plain to be seen in the sand. I stood like one thunderstruck, or as if I had seen an apparition. I listened, I looked round me; I could hear nothing, nor see anything. I went up to a rising ground to look farther. I went up the shore and down the shore; but it was all one, I could see no other impression but that one. I went to it again to see if there were any more, and to observe if it might not be my fancy, but there was no room for that, for there was exactly the very print of a foot, toes, heel, and every part of a foot — how it came thither I knew not, nor could in the least imagine. But after innumerable fluttering thoughts, like a man perfectly confused and out of myself, I came home to my fortification, not feeling, as we say, the ground I went on, but terrified to the last degree, looking behind me at every two or three steps, mistaking every bush and tree, and fancying every stump at a distance to be a man. Nor is it possible to describe how many various shapes affrighted imagination represented things to me in; how many wild ideas were found every moment in my fancy, and what strange unaccountable whimsies came into my thoughts by the way.

When I came to my castle, for so I think I called it ever after this, I fled into it like one pursued. Whether I went over by the ladder as first contrived, or went in at the hole in the rock which I called a door, I cannot remember; no, nor did I remember the next morning; for never a frighted hare fled to cover, nor fox to earth, with more terror of mind than I to this retreat.

CHAPTER TWELVE

I slept none that night. The farther I was from the occasion of my fright the greater my apprehensions were, which is something contrary to the nature of such things, and especially to the usual practice of all creatures in fear. But I was so embarrassed with my own frightful ideas of the thing, that I formed nothing but dismal imaginations to myself, even though I was now a great way off it. Sometimes I fancied it must be the devil; and reason joined in with me upon this supposition. For how should any other thing in human shape come into the place? Where was the vessel that brought them? What marks were there of any other footsteps? And how was it possible a man should come there?

I presently concluded that it must be some of the savages of the mainland over against me, who had wandered out to sea in their canoes, and either driven by the currents, or by contrary winds, had made the island; and had been on shore, but were gone away again to sea, being as loath, perhaps, to have stayed in this desolate island as I would have been to have had them.

While these reflections were rolling upon my mind, I was very thankful in my thoughts that I was so happy as not to be thereabouts at that time, or that they did not see my boat, by which they would have concluded that some inhabitants had been in the place, and perhaps have searched farther for me. Then terrible thoughts racked my imagination about their having found my boat, and that there were people here; and that if so, I should certainly have them come again in greater numbers and devour me; that if it should happen so that they should not find me, yet they would find my enclosure, destroy all my corn, carry away all my flock of tame goats, and I should perish at last for mere want.

In the middle of these cogitations, apprehensions, and reflections, it came into my thought one day that all this foot might be a mere chimera of my own; and that this foot might be the print of my own foot when I came on shore from my boat. This cheered me up a little, too, and I began to persuade myself it was all a delusion; that it was nothing else but my own foot; and why might not I come that way from the boat as well as I was going that way to the boat?

Heartening myself therefore with the belief that this was nothing but the print of one of my own feet, and so I might be truly said to start at my own shadow, I began to go abroad again, and went to my country house to milk my flock; but to see with what fear I went forward, how often I looked behind me, how I was ready every now and then to lay down my basket and run for my life, it would have made any one have thought I was haunted with an evil conscience, or that I had been lately most terribly frightened, and so indeed I had.

However, as I went down thus two or three days, and having seen nothing, I began to be a little bolder, and to think there was really nothing in it but my own imagination. But I could not persuade myself fully of this till I should go down to the shore again and see this print of a foot, and measure it by my own, and see if there was any similitude of fitness, that I might be assured it was my own foot. But when I came to the place; **First**, it appeared evidently to me that when I laid up my boat I could not possibly be on shore anywhere thereabout. **Secondly,** when I came to measure the mark with my own foot, I found my foot not so large by a great deal. Both these things filled my head with new imaginations, and gave me the vapours again to the highest degree; so that I shook with cold like one in an ague. And I went home again, filled with the belief that some man or men had been on shore there; or, in short, that the island was inhabited, and I might be surprised before I was aware — and what course to take for my security I knew not.

This confusion of my thoughts kept me waking all night; but in the morning I fell asleep, and having by the amusement of my mind been as it were tired, and my spirits exhausted, I slept very soundly, and waked much better composed than I had ever been before; and now I began to think sedately. And upon the utmost debate with myself, I concluded. That this island, which was so exceeding pleasant, fruitful, and no farther from the mainland than I had seen, was not so entirely abandoned as I had imagined. That although there were no stated inhabitants who lived on the spot, yet that there might sometimes come boats off from the shore, who either with design, or perhaps never but when they were driven by cross winds, might come to this place.

That I had lived here fifteen years now, and had not met with the least shadow or figure of any people yet; and that if at any time they should be driven here, it was probable they went away again as soon as ever they could, seeing they had never thought fit to fix there upon any occasion, to this time.

That the most I could suggest any danger from was, from any such casual accidental landing of straggling people from the main who, as it was likely, if they were driven hither, were here against their wills; so they made no stay here but went off again with all possible speed, seldom staying one night on shore, lest they should not have the help of the tides and daylight back again; and that, therefore, I had nothing to do but to consider of some safe retreat, in case I should see any savages land upon the spot.

Now I began sorely to repent that I dug my cave so large as to bring a door through again; which door, as I said, came out beyond where my fortification joined to the rock. Upon maturely considering this, therefore, I resolved to draw me a second fortification, in the same manner of a semicircle, at a distance from my wall, just where I had planted a double row of trees about twelve years before, of which I made mention. These trees having been planted so thick before, they wanted but a few piles to be driven between them that they should be thicker and stronger, and my wall would be soon finished.

So that I had now a double wall, and my outer wall was thickened with pieces of timber, old cables, and everything I could think of to make it strong; having in it seven little holes about as big as I might put my arm out at. In the inside of this I thickened my wall to about ten foot thick, with continual bringing earth out of my cave and laying it at the foot of the wall and walking upon it; and through the seven holes I contrived to plant muskets, of which I took notice that I got seven on shore out of the ship; these, I say, I planted like my cannon, and fitted them into frames that held them like a carriage so that I could fire all the seven guns in two minutes' time. This wall I was many a weary month in finishing, and yet never thought myself safe till it was done.

When this was done I stuck all the ground without my wall, for a great way every way, as full with stakes or sticks of the osier-like wood, which I found so apt to grow, as they could well stand; insomuch that I believe I might set in near twenty thousand of them, leaving a pretty large space between them and my wall, that I might have room to see an enemy, and they might have no shelter from the young trees, if they attempted to approach my outer wall.

Thus in two years' time I had a thick grove, and in five or six years' time I had a wood before my dwelling, growing so monstrous thick and strong, that it was indeed perfectly impassable; and no men, of what kind soever, would ever imagine that there was anything beyond it, much less a habitation. As for the way which I proposed to myself to go in and out (for I left no avenue), it was by setting two ladders: one to a part of the rock which was low, and then broke in, and left room to place another ladder upon that. So, when the two ladders were taken down, no man living could come down to me without mischieving himself; and if they had come down, they were still on the outside of my outer wall.

This I took all the measures human prudence could suggest for my own preservation; and it will be seen at length that they were not altogether without just reason, though I foresaw nothing at that time more than my mere fear suggested to me.

While this was doing, I was not altogether careless of my other affairs; for I had a great concern upon me for my little herd of goats. They were not only a present supply to me upon every occasion, and began to be sufficient to me, without the expense of powder and shot, but also without the fatigue of hunting after the wild ones; and I was loath to lose the advantage of them, and to have them all to nurse up over again.

To this purpose, after long consideration, I could think of but two ways to preserve them: one was, to find another convenient place to dig a cave underground, and to drive them into it every night; and the other was, to enclose two or three little bits of land, remote from one another, and as much concealed as I could, where I might keep about half-a-dozen young goats in each place; so that, if any disaster happened to the flock in general, I might be able to raise them again with little trouble and time. And this, though it would require a great deal of time and labour, I thought was the most rational design.

Accordingly, I spent some time to find out the most retired parts of the island; and I pitched upon one which was as private indeed as my heart could wish for. It was a little damp piece of ground in the middle of the hollow and thick woods where, as is observed, I almost lost myself once before, endeavouring to come back that way from the eastern part of the island. Here I found a clear piece of land — near three acres — so surrounded with woods that it was almost an enclosure by nature; at least, it did not want near so much labour to make it so as the other pieces of ground I had worked so hard at.

I immediately went to work with this piece of ground; and in less than a month's time I had so fenced it round that my flock or herd — call it which you please — who were not so wild now as at first they might be supposed to be, were well enough secured in it. So, without any further delay, I removed ten young she-goats and two he-goats to this place; and when they were there, I continued to perfect the fence till I had made it as secure as the other; which, however, I did at more leisure and it took me up more time by a great deal.

All this labour was purely from my apprehension was account of the print of a man's foot which I had seen; for as yet I never saw any human creature come near the island, and I had now lived two years under these uneasinesses, which indeed made my life much less comfortable than it was before — as may well be imagined by any who know what it is to live in the constant snare of **the fear of man**.

After I had thus secured one part of my little living stock, I went about the whole island searching for another private place to make such another deposit, when, wandering more to the west point of the island than I had ever done yet, and looking out to sea, I thought I saw a boat upon the sea at a great distance. I had found a prospective-glass or two in one of the seamen's chests which I saved out of our ship; but I had it not about me, and this was so remote that I could not tell what to make of it, though I looked at it till my eyes were not able to hold to look any longer. Whether it was a boat or not, I do not know; but as I descended from the hill I could see no more of it; so I gave it over — only I resolved to go no more out without a prospective-glass in my pocket.

When I was come down the hill to the end of the island — where, indeed, I had never been before — I was presently convinced that the seeing of the print of a man's foot was not such a strange thing in the island as I imagined. And but that it was a special providence that I was cast upon the side of the island where the savages never came, I should easily have known that nothing was more frequent than for the canoes from the main, when they happened to be a little too far out at sea, to shoot over to that side of the island for harbour; likewise, as they often met and fought in their canoes, the victors having taken any prisoners would bring them over to the shore, where, according to their dreadful customs, being all cannibals, they would kill and eat them; of which hereafter.

When I was come down the hill to the shore, as I said above, being the south-west point of the island, I was perfectly confounded and amazed — not is it possible for me to express the horror of my mind — at seeing the shore spread with skulls, hands, feet, and other bones of human bodies; and particularly I observed a place where there had been a fire made, and a circle dug in the earth like a cockpit, where it is supposed the savage wretches had sat down to their inhuman feastings upon the bodies of their fellow-creatures.

I was so astonished with the sight of these things that I entertained no notions of any danger to myself from it for a long while. All my apprehensions were buried in the thoughts of such a pitch of inhuman hellish brutality, and the horror of the degeneracy of human nature; which though I had heard of often, yet I never had so near a view of before.

I entertained such an abhorrence of the savage wretches that I have been speaking of, and of the wretched inhuman custom of their devouring and eating one another up, that I continued pensive and sad, and kept close within my own circle for almost two years after this. When I say my own circle, I mean by it my three plantations — namely, my castle, my country seat, which I called my bower, and my enclosure in the woods. Nor did I look after this for any other use than as an enclosure for my goats; for the aversion which nature gave me to these hellish wretches was such that I was fearful of seeing them as of seeing the devil himself. Nor did I so much as go to look after my boat in all this time, but began rather to think of making me another; for I could not think of ever making any more attempts to bring the other boat round the island to me, lest I should meet with some of these creatures at sea, in which, if I had happened to have fallen into their hands, I knew what would have been my lot.

CHAPTER THIRTEEN

As in my present condition there were not really many things which I wanted, so indeed I thought that the frights I had been in about these savage wretches, and the concern I had been in for my own preservation, had taken off the edge of my invention for my own conveniences; and I had dropped a good design which I had once bent my thoughts too much upon, and that was to try if I could not make some of my barley into malt, and then try to brew myself some beer. This was really a whimsical thought, and I reproved myself often for the simplicity of it; for I presently saw there would be the want of several things necessary to the making my beer that it would be impossible for me to supply. As, first, casks to preserve it in; which was a thing that, as I have observed already, I could never compass — no, though I spent, not many days, but weeks, nay months , in attempting it, but to no purpose. In the next place, I had no hopes to make it keep, no yeast to make it work, no copper or kettle to make it boil. And yet all these things notwithstanding, I verily believe had not these things intervened — I mean the frights and terrors I was in about the savages — I had undertaken it, and perhaps brought it to pass too;

for I seldom gave anything over without accomplishing it, when I once had it in my head enough to begin with it.

But my invention now run quite another way; for night and day I could think of nothing but how I might destroy some of these monsters in their cruel, bloody entertainment, and, if possible, save the victim they should bring hither to destroy. It would take up a larger volume than this whole work is intended to be, to set down all the contrivances I hatched, or rather brooded upon in my thoughts, for the destroying these creatures, or at least frighting them, so as to prevent their coming hither any more. But all was abortive: nothing could be possible to take effect unless I was to be there to do it myself. And what could one man do among them when perhaps there might be twenty or thirty of them together, with their darts or their bows and arrows, with which they could shoot as true to a mark as I could with my gun?

Sometimes I contrived to dig a hole under the place where they made their fire, and put in five or six pounds of gunpowder, which when they kindled their fire would consequently take fire, and blow up all that was near it. But as, in the first place, I should be very loath to waste so much powder upon them, my store being now within the quantity of one barrel, so neither could I be sure of its going off at any certain time, when it might surprise them, and at best that it would do little more than just blow the fire about their ears and fright them, but not sufficient to make them forsake the place: so I laid it aside, and then proposed that I would place myself in ambush, in some convenient place, with my three guns all double-loaded, and in the middle of their bloody ceremony, let fly at them, when I should be sure to kill or wound perhaps two or three at every shot; and then falling in upon them with my three pistols and my sword, I made no doubt but that if there was twenty I should kill them all. This fancy pleased my thoughts for some weeks, and I was so full of it that I often dreamed of it, and sometimes that I was just going to let fly at them in my sleep.

Well, at length I found a place in the side of the hill, where I was satisfied I might securely wait till I saw any of their boats coming, and might then, even before they would be ready to come on shore, convey myself unseen into thickets of trees, in one of which there was a hollow large enough to conceal me entirely, and where I might sit and observe all their bloody doings, and take my full aim at their heads, when they were so close together as that it would be next to impossible that I should miss my shoot, or that I could fail wounding three or four of them at the first shoot.

In this place, then, I resolved to fix my design, and accordingly I prepared two muskets and my ordinary fowling-piece. The two muskets I loaded with a brace of slugs each, and four or five smaller bullets, about the size of pistol bullets; and the fowling-piece I loaded with near a handful of swan-shot, of the largest size; I also loaded my pistols with about four bullets each, and in this posture, well provided with ammunition for a second and third charge, I prepared myself for my expedition.

After I had thus laid the scheme of my design, and in my imagination put it in practice, I continually made my tour every morning up to the top of the hill, which was from my castle, as I called it, about three miles, or more, to see if I could observe any boats upon the sea, coming near the island, or standing over towards it. But I began to tire of this hard duty, after I had for two or three months constantly kept my watch, but come always back without any discovery, there having not in all that time been the least appearance, not only on or near the shore, but not on the whole ocean, so far as my eyes or glasses could reach every way.

As long as I kept up my daily tour to the hill to look out, so long also I kept up the vigour of my design, and my spirits seemed to be all the while in a suitable form for so outrageous an execution as the killing twenty or thirty naked savages, for an offence which I had not at all entered into a discussion in my thoughts, any farther than my passions were at first fired by the horror I conceived at the unnatural custom of that people of the country, who it seems had been suffered by Providence, in his wise disposition of the world, to have no other guide than that of their own abominable and vitiated passions; and consequently were left, and perhaps had been so for some ages, to act such horrid things, and receive such dreadful customs, as nothing but nature entirely abandoned of Heaven and acted by some hellish degeneracy, could have run them into. But now, when, as I have said, I began to be weary of the fruitless excursion which I had made so long, and so far, every morning in vain, so my opinion of the action itself began to alter, and I began with cooler and calmer thoughts to consider what it was I was going to engage in; — what authority or call I had to pretend to be judge and executioner upon these men as criminals, whom Heaven had thought fit for so many ages to suffer unpunished, to go on, was a kind of hollow place. I was curious to look into it, and getting with difficulty into the mouth of it, I found it was pretty large; that is to say, sufficient for me to stand upright in it, and perhaps another with me. But I must confess to you I made more haste out than I did in, when looking farther into the place, and which was perfectly dark, I saw two broad shining eyes of some creature, whether devil or man I knew not, which twinkled like two stars, the dim light from the cave's mouth shining directly in and making the reflection.

However, after some pause, I recovered myself, and began to call myself a thousand fools, and tell myself that he that was afraid to see the devil was not fit to live twenty years in an island all alone; and that I durst to believe there was nothing in this cave that was more frightful than myself. Upon this, plucking up my courage, I took up a great firebrand and in I rushed again, with the stick flaming in my hand. I had not gone three steps in but I was almost as much frighted as I was before; for I heard a very loud sigh, like that of a man in some pain; and it was followed by a broken noise, as if of words half-expressed, and then a deep sigh again. I stepped back, and was indeed struck with such a surprise that it put me into a cold sweat; and if I had had a hat on my head, I will not answer for it that my hair might not have lifted it off! But still, plucking up my spirits as well as I could, and encouraging myself a little with considering that the power and presence of God was everywhere, and was able to protect me, upon this, stepped forward again, and by the light of the brand, holding it up a little over my head, I

and to be, as it were, the executioners of his judgments one upon another. How far these people were offenders against me, and what right I had to engage in the quarrel of that blood, which they shed promiscuously one upon another. I debated very often with myself thus: How do I know what God Himself judges in this particular case? It is certain these people do not commit it in defiance of divine justice, as we do in almost all the sins we commit. They think it no more a crime to kill a captive taken in war, than we do to kill an ox; nor to eat human flesh, than we do to eat mutton.

Upon the whole, I concluded, that neither in principles nor in policy I ought one way or other to concern myself in this affair; — that my business was by all possible means to conceal myself from them, and not to leave the least signal to them to guess by that there were any living creatures upon the island, — I mean of human shape.

In this disposition I continued for near a year after this, and so far was I from desiring an occasion for falling upon these wretches, that in all that time I never once went up the hill to see whether there were any of them in sight, or to know whether any of them had been on shore there or not, that I might not be tempted to renew any of my contrivances against them, or be provoked by any advantage which might present itself, to fall upon them, only this I did, I went and removed my boat, which I had on the other side of the island, and carried it down to the east end of the whole island, where I ran it into a little cove which I found under some high rocks, and where I knew, by reason of the currents, the savages durst not, at least would not, come with their boats upon any account whatsoever

With my boat I carried away every thing that I had left there belonging to her, though not necessary for the bare going thither — namely, a mast and sail which I had made for her, and a thing like an anchor, but indeed which could not be called either anchor or grapling — however, it was the best I could make of its kind. All these I removed, that there might not be the least shadow of any discovery, or any appearance of any boat or of any human habitation upon the island.

Besides this, I kept myself, as I said, more retired than before, and seldom went from my cell, other than upon my constant employment — namely, to milk my she-goats and manage my little flock in the wood; which, as it was quite on the other part of the island, was quite out of danger; for certain it is, that these savage people who sometimes haunted this island, never came with any thoughts of finding anything here, and consequently never wandered off from the coast. And I doubt not but they might have been several times on shore after my apprehensions of them had made me cautious as well as before; and indeed, I looked back with some horror upon the thoughts of what my condition would have been, if I had chopped upon them, and been discovered, before that, when naked and unarmed, except for one gun, and that loaded only with small shot.

I believe the reader of this will not think strange if I confess that these anxieties, these constant dangers I lived in, and the concern that was now upon me, put an end to all invention and to all the contrivances that I had laid for my future accommodations and conveniences. I had the care of my safety more now upon my hands than that of my food. I cared not to drive a nail or chop a stick of wood now, for fear the noise I should make should be heard; much less would I fire a gun, for the same reason. And above all, I was intolerably uneasy at making any fire, lest the smoke, which is visible at a great distance in the day, should betray me; and for this reason I removed that part of my business, which required fire, such as burning of pots and pipes, & c., into my new apartment in the woods, where, after I had been some time, I found to my unspeakable consolation a mere natural cave in the earth, which went in a vast way, and where, I dare say, no savage, had he been at the mouth of it, would be so hardy as to venture in, nor indeed would any man else; but one who, like me, wanted nothing so much as a safe retreat.

The mouth of this hollow was at the bottom of a great rock, where, by mere accident (I would say if I did not see abundant reason to ascribe all su things now to Providence), I was cutting do some thick branches of trees to make charcoal. before I go on I must observe the reason o making this charcoal, which was thus:

I was afraid of making a smoke about m tation, as I said before; and yet I could not li without baking my bread, cooking my m So I contrived to burn some wood here seen done in England, under turf, till chark, or dry coal; and then putting th preserved the coal to carry home and other services which fire was wantin without danger of smoke.

But this by-the-by. While I w some wood here, I perceived tha thick branch of low brushwood o

saw lying on the ground a most monstruous frightful old he-goat, just making his will, as we say, and
gasping for life, and dying indeed of mere old age.

I stirred him a little to see if I could get him
out, and he essayed to get up, but was not able to
raise himself. And I thought with myself he might
even lie there; for if he had frighted me so, he
would certainly fright any of the savages, if any
of them should be so hardy as to come in there
while he had any life in him.

I was now recovered from my surprise, and
began to look round me, when I found the cave was
but very small; that is to say, it might be about
twelve foot over, but in no manner of shape, either
round or square, no hands having ever been employed in making it, but those of mere Nature. I observed also that there was a place at the farther side
of it that went in farther, but was so low that it
required me to creep upon my hands and knees to
go into it, and whither I went I know not. So,
having no candle, I gave it over for some time, but
resolved to come again the next day, provided with
candles and a tinder-box.

Accordingly, the next day I came provided with
six large candles of my own making — for I made
very good candles now of goat's tallow — and going
into this low place, I was obliged to creep upon all
fours, as I have said, almost ten yards; which, by
the way, I thought as a venture bold enough, considering that I knew not how far it might go, nor
what was beyond it. When I was got through the
strait I found the roof rose higher up — I believe
near twenty foot. But never was such a glorious
sight seen in the island, I dare say, as it was to look
round the sides and roof of this vault or cave. The

walls reflected a hundred thousand lights to me from my two candles. What it was in the rock, whether diamonds or any other precious stones, or gold, which I rather supposed it to be, I knew not.

The place I was in was most delightful cavity or grotto of its kind as could be expected, though perfectly dark. The floor was dry and level, and had a sort of small loose gravel upon it, so that there was no nauseous or venomous creature to be seen, neither was there any damp or wet on the sides or roof. The only difficulty in it was the entrance, which, however, as it was a place of security, and such a retreat as I wanted, I thought that was a convenience, so that I was really rejoiced at the discovery, and resolved without any delay to bring some of those things which I was most anxious about to this place. Particularly, I resolved to bring hither my magazine of powder and all my spare arms — namely, two fowling pieces, for I had three in all; and three muskets, for of them I had eight in all. So I kept at my castle only five, which stood ready mounted, like pieces of cannon, on my outmost fence, and were ready also to take out upon any expedition.

Upon this occasion of removing my ammunition, I took occasion, to open the barrel of powder which I took up out of the sea, and which had been wet; and I found that the water had penetrated about three or four inches into the powder on every side, which, caking and growing hard, had preserved the inside like a kernel in a shell. So that I had near sixty pounds of very good powder in the centre of the cask, and this was an agreeable discovery to me at that time. So I carried all away thither, never keeping above two or three pound of powder with me in my castle for fear of a surprise of any kind. I also carried thither all the lead I had left, for bullets.

I fancied myself now like one of the ancient giants, which were said to live in caves and holes in the rocks, where none could come at them. For I persuaded myself, while I was here, if five hundred savages were to hunt me, they could never find me out; or if they did, they would not venture to attack me here.

The old goat, who I found expiring, died in the mouth of the cave the next day after I made this discovery; and I found it much easier to dig a great hole there, and throw him in and cover him with earth, than to drag him out. So I interred him there to prevent offence to my nose.

CHAPTER FOURTEEN

It was now the month of December, in my twenty-third year; when going out pretty early in the morning, even before it was thorough daylight, I was surprised with seeing a light of some fire upon the shore, at a distance from me of about two mile, towards the end of the island where I had observed some savages had been as before; but not on the other side, but, to my great affliction, it was on my side of the island.

In this extremity, I went back directly to my castle, pulled up the ladder after me, and made all things without look as wild and natural as I could.

Then I prepared myself within, putting myself in a posture of defence. I loaded all my cannon, as I called them — that is to say, my muskets, which were mounted upon my new fortification — and all my pistols, and resolved to defend myself to the last gasp. And in this posture, I continued about two hours, but began to be mighty impatient for intelligence abroad, for I had no spies to send out.

After sitting a while longer, and musing what I should do in this case, I was not able to bear sitting in ignorance any longer; so setting up my ladder to the side of the hill, where there was a flat place, as I observed before, and then pulling the ladder up after me, I set it up again, and mounted to the top of the hill, and pulling out my perspective-glass, which I had taken on purpose, I laid me down flat on my belly on the ground, and began to look for the place. I presently found there was no less than nine naked savages, sitting round a small fire they had made.

They had two canoes with them, which they had hauled up 'upon the shore; and as it was then tide of ebb, they seemed to me to wait for the return of the flood to go away again. It is not easy to imagine what confusion this sight put me into, especially seeing them come on my side the island, and so near me too; but when I observed their coming must be always with the current of the ebb, I began afterwards to be more sedate in my mind, being satisfied that I might go abroad with safety all the time of the tide of flood, if they were not on shore before. And having made this observation, I went abroad about my harvest-work with the more composure.

As I expected, so it proved; for as soon as the tide made to the westward, I saw them all take boat, and row, or paddle, as we call it, all away. I should have observed that for an hour and more before they went off they went to dancing, and I could easily discern their postures and gestures by my glasses. I could not perceive, by my nicest observation, but that they were stark naked, and had not the least covering upon them; but whether they were men or women, that I could not distinguish.

As soon as I saw them shipped and gone, I took two guns upon my shoulders, and two pistols at my girdle, and my great sword by my side, without a scabbard, and with all the speed I was able to make, I went away to the hill where I had discovered the first appearance of all; and as soon as I got hither, which was not less than two hours (for I could not go apace, being so laden with arms as I was), I perceived there had been three canoes more of savages on that place; and looking out farther, I saw they were all at sea together, making over for the main.

This was a dreadful sight to me, especially when, going down to the shore, I could see the marks of horror which the dismal work they had been about and left behind it — namely, the blood, the bones, and part of the flesh of human bodies, eaten and devoured by those wretches with merriment and sport.

I spent my days now in great perplexity and anxiety of mind, expecting that I should one day or other fall into the hands of these merciless creatures; and if I did at any time venture abroad, it was not without looking round me with the greatest care and caution imaginable. And now I found to my great comfort how happy it was that I provided for a tame flock or herd of goats; for I durst not upon any account fire my gun, especially near that side of the island where they usually came, lest I should alarm the savages; and if they had fled from me now, I was sure to have them come back again, with perhaps two or three hundred canoes with them, in a few days, and then I knew what to expect.

However, I wore out a year and three months more before I ever saw any more of the savages, and then I found them again, as I shall soon observe. It is true that they might have been there once or twice, but either they made no stay, or at least I did not hear them; but in the month of May, as near as I could calculate, and in my four-and-twentieth year, I was surprised with a noise of a gun, as I thought, fired at sea.

This was, to be sure, a surprise of a quite different nature from any I had met with before. I started up in the greatest haste imaginable, and in a trice clapped my ladder to the middle place of the rock, and pulled it after me, and mounting it the second time, got to the top of the hill, the very moment that a flash of fire bid me listen for a second gun, which accordingly in about half a minute I heard, and by the sound knew that it was from that part of the sea where I was driven down the current in my boat.

I immediately considered that must be some ship in distress, and that they had some comrade or some other ship in company, and fired these guns for signals of distress and to obtain help. I had this presence of mind at that minute as to think that though I could not help them, it may be they might help me; so I brought together all the dry woods I could get at hand, and making a good handsome pile, I set it on fire upon the hill. The wood was dry and blazed freely, and though the wind blew very hard, yet it burned fairly out, that I was certain if there was any such things as a ship they must needs see it; and no doubt they did, for as soon as ever my fire blazed up I heard another gun, and after that several others, all from the same quarter. I plied my fire all night long till day broke; and when it was broad day, and the air cleared up, I saw something at a great distance at sea, full east of the island, whether a sail or a hull I could not distinguish, the distance was so great, and the weather still something hazy.

I looked frequently at it all that day, and soon perceived that it did not move; so I presently concluded that it was a ship and being eager, you may be sure, to be satisfied, I took my gun in hand, and ran toward the south side of the island to the rocks where I had formerly been carried away with the current; and getting up there, the weather by this time being perfectly clear, I could plainly see, to my great sorrow, the wreck of a ship cast away in the night upon those concealed rocks which I found when I was out in my boat.

Until the last year of my being on this island, I never knew whether any were saved out of that ship or no; and had only the affliction some days after, to see the corpse of a drowned boy come on shore, at the end of the island which was next the shipwreck. He had on no clothes, but a seaman's waistcoat, a pair of open-kneed linen drawers, and a blue linen shirt; but nothing to direct me so much as to guess what nation he was of. He had nothing in his pocket but two pieces of eight and a tobacco pipe. The last was to me of ten times more value than the first.

It was now calm, and I had a great mind to venture out in my boat to this wreck; not doubting that I might find something on board that might be useful to me. But that did not altogether press me so much as the possibility that there might be yet some living creature on board, whose life I might not only save, but might, by saving that life, comfort my own to the last degree; and this thought clung so to my heart that I could not be quiet, night nor day, but I must venture out in my boat on board this wreck.

Under the power of this impression, I hastened back to my castle, prepared everything for my voyage, took a quantity of bread, a great pot for fresh water, a compass to steer by, a bottle of rum, — for I had still a great deal of that left, — a basket full of raisins. And thus loading myself with everything necessary, I went down to my boat, got the water out of her, and got her afloat.

I resolved the next morning to set out with the first tide. I made first a little out to sea full north, till I began to feel the benefit of the current, which set eastward, and which carried me at a great rate, and yet did not so hurry me as the southern side current had done before, and so as to take from me all government of the boat; but having a strong steerage with my paddle, I went at a great rate, directly for the wreck, and in less than two hours I came up to it.

It was a dismal sight to look at. The ship, which by its building was Spanish, stuck fast, jammed in between two rocks; all the stern and quarter of her was beaten to pieces with the sea; and as her forecastle, which stuck in the rocks, had run on with great violence, her mainmast and foremast were brought by the board — that is to say, broken short off. When I came close to her, a dog appeared upon her, who, seeing me coming, yelped and cried; and as soon as I called him, jumped into the sea to come to me, and I took him into the boat, but found him almost dead for hunger and thirst. I gave him a cake of my bread, and he ate it like a ravenous wolf that had been starving a fortnight in the snow. I then gave the poor creature some fresh water, with which if I would have let him, he would have burst himself.

After this I went on board; but the first sight I met with was two men drowned in the forecastle of the ship, with their arms fast about one another. I concluded, as is indeed probable, that when the ship struck, it being in a storm, the sea broke so high and so continually over her, that the men were not able to bear it, and were strangled with the constant rushing in of the water, as much as if they had been under water. Besides the dog, there was nothing left in the ship that had life; nor any goods that I could see, but what were spoiled by the water. There were some casks of liquor — whether wine or brandy, I knew not — which lay lower in the hold, and which, the water being ebbed out, I could see; but they were too big to meddle with. I saw several chests, which I believed belonged to some of the seamen, and I got two of them into the boat, without examining what was in them.

Had the stern of the ship been fixed and the forepart broken off, I am persuaded I might have made a good voyage; for by what I found in these two chests, I had room to suppose the ship had a great deal of wealth on board; and if I may guess by the course she steered, she must have been bound from the Buenos Ayres or the Rio de la Plata, in the south part of America, beyond the Brazils, to the Havannah, in the gulf of Mexico, and so, perhaps to Spain. She had, no doubt, a great treasure in her, but of no use at that time to anybody; and what became of the rest of her people I then knew not.

I found, besides these chests, a little cask full of liquor, of about twenty gallons, which I got into my boat with much difficulty. There were several muskets in the cabin and a great powder-horn, with about four pounds of powder in it. As for the muskets, I had no occasion for them — so I left them; but took the powder-horn. I took a fire-shovel and tongs, which I wanted extremely; as also two little brass kettles, a copper pot to make chocolate, and a gridiron. And with this cargo and the dog I came away, the tide beginning to make home again. And the same evening about an hour within night, I reached the island again, weary and fatigued to the last degree.

I reposed that night in the boat, and in the morning I resolved to harbour what I had gotten in my new cave, not to carry it home to my castle. After refreshing myself, I got all my cargo on shore, and began to examine the particulars. The cask of liquor I found to be a kind of rum, but not such as we had at the Brazils — and, in a word, not at all good; but when I came to open the chests, I found several things of great use to me. For example, I found in one a fine case of bottles, of an extraordinary kind, and filled with cordial waters, fine, and very good; the bottles held about three pints each, and were tipped with silver; I found two pots of very good succades, or sweetmeats, so fastened also on top that the salt water had not hurt them; and two more of the same which the water had spoiled. I found some very good shirts, which were very welcome to me, and about a dozen and a half of linen white handkerchiefs, and coloured neckcloths — the former were also very welcome, being exceeding refreshing to wipe my face in a hot day; besides this, when I came to the till in the chests, I found there three great bags of pieces of eight, which held about eleven hundred pieces in all; and in one of them, wrapped up in a paper, six doubloons of gold, and some small bars of wedges of gold; I suppose they might all weigh near a pound.

Having now brought all my things on shore and secured them, I went back to my boat, and rowed or paddled her along the shore to her old harbour, where I laid her up and made the best of my way to my old habitation, where I found everything safe and quiet: so I began to repose myself, live after my old fashion, and take care of my family affairs; and for a while I lived easy enough; only that I was more vigilant than I used to be, looked out oftener, and did not go abroad so much; and if at any time I did stir with any freedom, it was always to the east part of the island, where I was pretty well satisfied the savages never came, and where I could go without so many precautions, and such a load of arms and ammunition, as I always carried with me if I went the other way.

I lived in this condition near two years more. But my unlucky head, that was always to let me know it was born to make my body miserable, was all the two years filled with project and designs how, if it were possible, I might get away from this island; for sometimes I was for making another voyage to the wreck, though my reason told me there was nothing left there worth the hazard of my voyage; sometimes for a ramble one way, sometimes another; and I believe verily, if I had had the boat that I went from Sallee in, I should have ventured to sea, bound anywhere, I knew not whither.

About a year and a half after I had entertained these notions, and by long musing had, as it were, resolved them all into nothing for want of an occasion to put them in execution, I was surprised one morning early with seeing no less than five canoes all on shore together on my side of the island and the people who belonged to them all landed and out of my sight! The number of them broke all my measures; for seeing so many, and knowing that they always came four or six, or sometimes more, in a boat, I could not tell what to think of it, or how to take my measures to attack tweny or thirty men single-handed; so I lay still in my castle, perplexed and discomforted. However, I put myself into all the same postures for an attack that I had formerly provided, and was just ready for action if anything had presented. Having waited a good while, listening to hear if they made any noise, at length, being very impatient, I set my guns at the foot of my ladder, and clambered up to the top of the hill by my two stages, as usual; standing so, howewer, that my head did not appear above the hill, so that they could not perceive me by any means. Here I observed, by the help of my perspective-glass, that they were no less than thirty in number, that they had a fire kindled, that they had had meat dressed. How they had cooked it, that I knew not, or what it was;

but they were all dancing, in I know not how many barbarous gestures and figures, their own way round the fire.

While I was thus looking on them, I perceived by my perspective two miserable wretches dragged from the boats, where it seems they were laid by, and were now brought out for the slaughter. I perceived one of them immediately fell, being knocked down, I suppose, with a club or wooden sword.

In that very moment, the other poor wretch, seeing himself a little at liberty, nature inspired him with hopes of life, and he started away from them, and ran with incredible swiftness along the sands directly towards me; I mean towards that part of the coast where my habitation was.

CHAPTER FIFTEEN

I was dreadfully frighted, that I must acknowledge, when I perceived him to run my way; and especially when, as I thought, I saw him pursued by the whole body. However, I kept my station, and my spirits began to recover when I found that there were not above three men that followed him; and still more was I encouraged, when I found that he outstripped them exceedingly in running, and gained ground of them, so that if he could but hold it for half an hour, I saw easily he would fairly get away from them all.

There was between them and my castle the creek, and this I saw plainly he must necessarily swim over, or the poor wretch would be taken there. But when the savage escaping came thither, he made nothing of it, though the tide was then up, but plunging in, swam through in about thirty strokes or thereabouts, landed and ran on with exceeding strength and swiftness. When the three persons came to the creek, I found that two of them could swim, but the third could not, and that standing on the other side, he looked at the other, but went no farther; and soon after went softly back again, which, as it happened, was very well for him in the main.

I observed that the two who swam were yet more than twice as long swimming over the creek as the fellow was that fled from them. It came now very warmly upon my thoughts, and indeed irresistibly, that now was my time to get me a servant, and perhaps a companion or assistant; and that I was called plainly by Providence to save this poor creature's life. I immediately ran down the ladders with all possible expedition, fetched my two guns, for they were both at the foot of the ladders, as I observed above; and getting up again with the same haste to the top of the hill, I crossed towards the sea; and having a very short cut and all down hill, clapped myself in the way between the pursuers and the pursued; hallooing aloud to him that fled, who, looking back, was at first perhaps as much frighted at me as at them: but I beckoned with my hand to him to come back; and, in the meantime, I slowly advanced toward the two that followed; then rushing at once upon the foremost, I knocked him down with the stock of my piece. I was loath to fire, because I would not have the rest hear; though at that distance it would not have been easily heard, and being out of sight of the smoke too, they would not have easily known what to make of it. Having knocked this fellow down, the other who pursued with him stopped, as if he had been frighted, and I advanced apace towards him; but as I came nearer, I perceived presently he had a bow and arrow, and was fitting it to shoot at me; so I was then necessitated to shoot at him first, which I did and killed him at the first shot. The poor savage who fled, but had stopped, though he saw both his enemies fallen, and killed, as he thought, yet was so frighted with the fire and noise of my piece, that he stood stock still, and neither came forward nor went backward, though he seemed rather inclined to fly still than to come on. I beckoned him again to come to me, and gave him all the signs of encouragement that I could think of, and he came nearer and nearer, kneeling down every ten or twelve steps in token of acknowledgement for my saving his life. I smiled at him, and looked pleasantly, and beckoned to him to come still nearer. At length he came to me, and then he kneeled down again, kissed the ground, and laid his head upon the ground, and taking me by the foot, set my foot upon his head; this, it seems, was in token of swearing to be my slave for ever. I took him up and made much of him, and encouraged him all I could. But there was more work to do yet; for I perceived the savage whom I knocked down was not killed, but stunned, with the blow, and I began to see he had come to himself; so I pointed to him, and showing him the savage, that he was not dead. Upon this he spoke some words to me, and though I could not understand them yet I thought they were pleasant to hear, for they were the first sound of a man's voice that I had heard, my own excepted, for above twenty-five years. But there was no time for such reflections now. The savage who was knocked down recovered himself so far as to sit up upon the ground, and I perceived that my savage began to be afraid; but when I saw that, I presented my other piece to the man, as if I would shoot him. Upon this my savage, for so I called him now, made a motion to me to lend him my sword, which hung naked in a belt by my side, so I did. He no sooner had it, but he runs to his enemy, and at one blow cut off his head so cleverly, no executioner in Germany could have done it sooner or better; which I thought very strange for one who I had reason to believe never saw a sword in his life before, except their own wooden swords. However, it seems, as I learned afterwards, they made their wooden swords so sharp, so heavy, and the wood so hard, that they will cut off heads even with them, ay, and arms, and that at one blow too. When he had done this, he comes laughing to me in sign of triumph, and brought me the sword again, and with abundance of gestures, which I did not understand, laid it down with the head of the savage that he had killed just before me.

But what astonished him most, was to know how I had killed the other Indian so far off. So pointing to him, he made signs to me to let him go to him; so I bade him go as well as I could. When he came to him he stood like one amazed, looking at him, turned him first on one side, then on the other, looked at the wound the bullet had made, which it seems was just in his breast, where it had made a hole, and no great quantity of blood had followed; but he had bled inwardly for he was quite dead. He took up his bow and arrows and came back, so I turned to go away, and beckoned to him to follow me, making signs to him that more might come after them.

Upon this he signed to me that he should bury them with sand, that they might not be seen by the rest if they followed; and so I made signs again to him to do so. He fell to work, and in an instant he had scraped a hole in the sand with hands, big enough to bury the first in, and then dragged him into it, and covered him, and did so also by the other. I believe he had buried them both in a quarter of an hour. Then calling him away I carried him, not to my castle, but quite away to my cave, on the farther part of the island.

Here I gave him bread and a bunch of raisins to eat, and a draught of water, which I found he was indeed in great distress for by his running. And having refreshed him, I made signs for him to go lie down and sleep, pointing to a place where I had laid a great parcel of rice straw, and a blanket upon it, which I used to sleep upon myself sometimes; so the poor creature lay down and went to sleep.

He was a comely, handsome fellow, perfectly well made, with straight strong limbs, not too large, tall and well shaped, and I reckon, about twenty-six years of age. He had a very good countenance, not a fierce and surly aspect; but seemed to have something very manly in his face; and yet he had all the sweetness and softness of an European in his countenance too, especially when he smiled. His hair was long and black, not curled like wool; his forehead very high and large, and a great vivacity and sparkling sharpness in his eyes. The colour of his skin was not quite black, but very tawny. His face was round and plump; his nose small, not flat like a negro's; a very good mouth, thin lips, and his fine teeth well set, and white as ivory.

After he had slumbered, rather than slept, about half an hour, he waked again, and comes out of the cave to me, for I had been milking my goats, which I had in the enclosure just by. In a little while I began to speak to him, and teach him to speak to me. And first, I made him know his name should be Friday, which was the day I saved his life. I likewise taught him to say Master, and then let him know that was to be my name. I likewise taught him to say Yes and No, and to know the meaning of them. I gave him some milk in an earthen pot, and let him see me drink it before him, and sop my bread in it. And I gave him a cake of bread to do the like, which he quickly complied with, and made signs that it was very good for him.

I kept there with him all that night; but as soon as it was day I beckoned to him to come with me, and let him know I would give him some clothes; at which he seemed very glad, for he was stark naked.

I then led him up to the top of the hill, to see if his enemies were gone; and, pulling out my glass, I looked and saw plainly the place where they had been, but no appearance of them or of their canoes; so that it was plain that they were gone, and had left their two comrades behind them, without any search for them.

But I was not content with this discovery; but having now more courage, and consequently more curiosity, I take my man Friday with me, giving him the sword in his hand with the bow and arrows at his back, which I found he could use very dexterously, making him carry one gun for me, and I two for myself, and away we marched to the place where these creatures had been, for I had a mind now to get some fuller intelligence of them. When I came to the place, my very blood ran chill in my veins, and my heart sank within me at the horror of the spectacle. Indeed it was a dreadful sight — at least it was so to me; though Friday made nothing of it. The place was covered with human bones, the ground dyed with their blood, great pieces of flesh left here and there, half-eaten, mangled and scorched; and, in short, all the tokens of the triumphant feast they had been making there, after a victory over their enemies.

I caused Friday to gather all the skulls, bones, flesh, and whatever remained, and lay them together on a heap, and make a great fire upon it, and burn them all to ashes.

When we had done this, we came back to our castle, and there I fell to work for my man Friday; and first of all I gave him a pair of linen drawers, which I found in the wreck, and which with a little alteration fitted him very well. Then I made him a jerkin of goat-skin, as well as my skill would allow, and I was now grown a tolerable good tailor; and I gave him a cap which I had made of a hare-skin, very convenient and fashionable enough; and thus he was clothed for the present tolerably well, and was mighty well pleased to see himself almost as well clothed as his master. It is true, he went awkwardly in these things at first; wearing the drawers was very awkward to him, and the sleeves of the waistcoat galled his shoulders and the inside of his arms; but a little easing them where he complained they hurt him, and using himself to them, at length he took to them very well.

The next day after I came home to my hutch with him, I began to consider where I should lodge him; and that I might do well for him, and yet be perfectly easy myself, I made a little tent for him in the vacant place between my two fortifications, in the inside of the last, and in the outside of the first. And as there was a door or entrance there into my cave, I made a formal framed doorcase, and a door to it of boards, and set it up in the passage, a little within the entrance; and causing the door to open on the inside, I barred it up in the night, taking in my ladders too; so that Friday could no way come at me in the inside of my innermost wall without making so much noise in getting over, that it must needs waken me. For my first wall had now a complete roof over it of long poles covering all my tent and leaning up to the side of the hill, which was again laid cross with smaller sticks instead of laths, and then thatched over a great thickness with the rice straw, which was strong like reeds; and at the hole or place which was left to go in or out by the ladder, I had placed a kind of trap-door, which, if it had been attempted on the outside, would not have opened at all, but would have fallen down and made a great noise; and as to weapons, I took them all in to my side every night.

But I needed none of all this precaution; for never man had a more faithful, loving, sincere servant than Friday was to me; without passions, sullenness, or designs, perfectly obliged and engaged; his very affections were tied to me, like those of a child to a father, and I dare say he would have sacrificed his life for the saving mine upon any occasion whatsoever. The many testimonies he gave me of this, put it out of doubt, and soon convinced me that I needed to use no precautions as to my safety on his account.

After I had been two or three days returned to my castle, I thought that, in order to bring Friday off his horrid way of feeding, and from the relish of a cannibal's stomach, I ought to let him taste other flesh; so I took him out with me one morning to the woods. I went, indeed, intending to kill a kid out of my own flock, and bring him home and dress it; but, as I was going, I saw a she-goat lying down in the shade, and two young kids sitting by her, I catched hold of Friday. "Hold," says I, "stand still," and made signs to him not to stir. Immediately, I presented my piece, shot, and killed one of the kids. The poor creature, who had at a distance indeed seen me kill the savage his enemy, but did not know, or could imagine, how it was done, was sensibly surprised, trembled, and shook, and looked so amazed, that I thought he would have sunk down. He did not see the kid I had shot at, or perceive I had killed it, but ripped up his waistcoat to feel if he was not wounded, and, as I found, presently thought I was resolved to kill him; for he came and kneeled down to me, and embracing my knees, said a great many things I did not understand, but I could easily see that the meaning was to pray me not to kill him.

Well, after his astonishment was a little over at this, I brought home the kid, and the same evening, I took the skin off, and cut it out as well as I could; and having a pot for that purpose, I boiled or stewed some of the flesh, and made some very good broth;

and after I had begun to eat some, I gave some to my man, who seemed very glad of it, and liked it very well. But that which was strangest to him was to see me eat salt with it. He made a sign to me that the salt was not good to eat, and putting a little into his own mouth he seemed to nauseate it, and would spit and splutter at it, washing his mouth with fresh water after it.

Having thus fed him with boiled meat and broth, I was resolved to feast him the next day with roasting a piece of the kid. This I did by hanging it before the fire in a string, as I had seen many people do in England, setting two poles up one on each side the fire, and one cross on the top, and tying the string to the cross-stick, letting the meat turn occasionally. This Friday admired very much; but when he came to taste the flesh, he took so many ways to tell me how well he liked it, that I could not but understand him; and at last he told me he would never eat man's flesh any more — which I was very glad to hear.

The next day I set him to work to beating some corn out, and sifting it in the manner I used to do, as I observed before; and he soon understood how to do it as well as I, especially after he had seen what the meaning of it was, and that it was to make bread of: for after that I let him see me make my bread, and bake it too, and in a little while Friday was able to do all the work for me, as well as I could do it myself.

I began now to consider that, having two mouths to feed instead of one, I must provide more ground for my harvest, and plant a larger quantity of corn than I used to do; so I marked out a larger piece of land, and began the fence in the same manner as before; in which Friday not only worked very willingly and very hard, but did it very cheerfully. And I told him what it was for; that it was for corn to make more bread, because he was now with me, and that I might have enough for him and myself too. He appeared very sensible of that part, and let me know that he thought I had much more labour upon me on his account than I had for myself; and that he would work the harder for me, if I would tell him what to do.

This was the pleasantest year of all the life I led in this place. Friday began to talk pretty well, and understand the names of almost everything I had occasion to call for, and of every place I had to send him to, and talk a great deal to me; so that, in short, I began now to have some use for my tongue again, which indeed I had very little occasion for before — that is to say, about speech. Besides the pleasure of talking to him, I had a singular satisfaction in the fellow himself. His simple unfeigned honesty appeared to me more and more every day, and I began really to love the creature; and, on his side, I believe he loved me more than it was possible for him ever to love anything before.

After Friday and I became more intimately acquainted, and that he could understand almost all I said to him, and speak fluently, though in broken English, to me, I acquainted him with my own story, or at least so much of it as related to my coming into the place, how I had lived there and how long. I let him into the mystery, for such it was to him, of gunpowder and bullet, and taught him how to shoot. I gave him a knife, which he was wonderfully delighted with; and I made him a belt, with a frog hanging to it, such as in England we wear hangers in; and in the frog, instead of a hanger, I gave him hatchet, which was not only as good a weapon in some cases, but much more useful upon other occasions.

I showed him the ruins of our boat which we lost when we escaped, and which I could not stir with my whole strength then, but was now almost fallen to pieces. Upon seeing this boat, Friday stood musing a great while, and said nothing. I asked him what it was he studied upon. At last says he, "Me see such boat like come to place at my nation."

Then I presently asked him if there were any white mans as he called them, in the boat.

"Yes," he said, "the boat full of white mans." I asked how many. He told upon his fingers seventeen. I asked him then what became of them. He told me, "They live, they dwell at my nation".

It was after this some considerable time, that being on the top of the hill, at the east side of the island, from whence, I had a clear day discovered the main, or continent, Friday looks very earnestly towards the mainland, and in a kind of surprise falls a jumping and dancing, and calls out to me, for I was at some distance from him. I asked him what was the matter. "Oh joy!" says he, "oh, glad! There see my country, there my nation!"

One day walking up the same hill, but the weather being hazy at sea, so the we could not see the continent, I called to him, and said, "Friday, do not you wish yourself in your own country, your own nation?"

"Yes," he said; "I be much O glad to be at my own nation."

I told him I would make him a canoe for him. He told me he would go if I would go with him.

"I go," says I; "Why, they will eat me if I come there."

"No, no," says he; "me make they no eat you; me make them love you."

He meant he would tell them how I had killed his enemies, and saved his life, and so he would make them love me. Then he told me as well as he could how kind they were to seventeen white men, or bearded men, as he called them, who came on shore there in distress.

From this time, I confess, I had a mind to venture over, and see if I could possibly join with these bearded men, who, I made no doubt, were Spaniards or Portuguese; not doubting but, if I could, we might find some method to escape from thence, being upon the continent, and a good company together, better than I could from an island forty miles off the shore and alone without help. So, after some days, I took Friday to work again, by way of discourse and told him I would give him a boat to go back to his own nation.

At last Friday pitched upon a tree, for I found he knew much better than I what kind of wood was fittest for it. Friday was for burning the hollow or cavity of this tree out to make it for a boat; but I showed him how rather to cut it out with tools; which, after I had showed him how to use, he did very handily; and in about a month's hard labour, we finished it, and made it very hansome, especially when with our axes, which I showed him how to handle, we cut and hewed the outside into the true shape of a boat. After this, however, it cost us near a fortnight's time to get her along, as it were, inch by inch, upon great rollers, into the water. But when she was in, she would have carried twenty men with great ease.

When she was in the water, and though she was so big, it amazed me to see with what dexterity and how swift my man Friday would manage her, turn her, and paddle her along; so I asked him if he would, and if we might venture over in her.

"Yes," he said; "he venture over in her very well, though great wind blow."

However, I had a further design that he knew nothing of; and that was, to make a mast and sail, and to fit her with an anchor and cable.

I was near two months performing this last work — namely, rigging and fitting my mast and sails; for I finished them very complete, making a small stay, and a sail or foresail to it, to assist if we should turn to windward. And, which was more than all, I fixed a rudder to the stern of her, to steer with.

CHAPTER SIXTEEN

I was now entered on the seven-and-twentieth year of my captivity in this place.

The rainy season was in the meantime upon me, when I kept more within doors than at other times. So I had stowed our new vessel as secure as we could, bringing her up into the creek where, as I said, in the beginning I landed my rafts from the ship; and hauling her up to the shore at high-water mark, I made my man Friday dig a little dock, just big enough to hold her, and just deep enough to give her water enough to float in: and then, when the tide was out, we made a strong dam accross the end of it, to keep the water out; and so she lay dry, as to the tide from the sea; and to keep the rain off, we laid a great many boughs of trees so thick that she was as well thatched as a house; and thus we waited for the months of November and December, in which I designed to make my adventure.

When the sattled season began to come in, I was preparing daily for the voyage. And the first thing I did was to lay by a certain quantity of provisions, being the stores for our voyage; and intended, in a week or a fortnight's time, to open the dock and launch out our boat. I was busy one morning upon something of this kind, when I called to Friday, and bid him go to the sea-shore and see if he could find a turtle or tortoise — a thing which we generally got once a week, for the sake of the eggs as well as the flesh. Friday had not been long gone, when he came running back, and flew over my outer wall or fence like one that felt not the ground or the steps he set his feet on; and before I had time to speak to him, he cries out to me, "O master! O master! — O sorrow! — O bad!"

"What's the matter, Friday?" says I.

"O — yonder — there," says he; "one, two, three canoe! — one, two, three!"

By his way of speaking I concluded there were six; but on enquiry, I found it was but three. "Well, Friday," says I, "do not be frighted." So I heartened him up as well as I could. However, I saw the poor fellow was most terribly scared; for nothing ran in his head but that they were come to look for him, and would cut him in pieces and eat him; and the poor fellow trembled so, that I scarce knew what to do with him. I comforted him as well as I could, and told him I was in as much danger as he was, and that they would eat me as well as him. "But," says I, "Friday, we must resolve to fight them. Can you fight, Friday?"

"Me shoot," says he; "but there come many great number."

"No matter for that," said I again; "our guns will fright them that we do not kill," so I asked him, whether, if I resolved to defend him, he would defend me, and stand by me, and do just as I bid him?

He said "Me die, when you bid die, master."

So I went and fetched a good dram of rum and gave him; for I had been so good a husband of my rum that I had a great deal left. When he had drank it, I made him take the two fowling-pieces, which we always carried and load them with large swan-shot, as big as small pistol bullets; then I took four muskets, and loaded them with two slugs and five small bullets, each; and my two pistols I loaded with a brace of bullets each; I hung my great sword as usual naked by my side, and gave Friday his hatchet.

When I had thus prepared myself, I took my perspective-glass, and went up to the side of the hill to see what I could discover. And I found quickly, by my glass, that there were one-and-twenty savages, three prisoners, and three canoes; and that their whole business seemed to be the triumphal banquet upon these three human bodies (a barbarous feast indeed), but nothing more than as I had observed was usual with them.

I observed, also that they were landed, not where they had done when Friday made his escape, but nearer to my creek, where the shore was low, and where a thick wood came close almost down to the sea. This, with the abhorrence of the inhuman errand those wretches came about, filled me with such indignation, that I came down again to Friday and told him I was resolved to go down to them and kill them all; and asked him if he would stand by me? He was now gotten over his fright, and his spirits being a little raised with the dram I had given him, he was very cheerful, and told me, as before, "he would die, when I bid die."

In this fit of fury, I took first and divided the arms which I had charged as before, between us. I gave Friday one pistol to stick in his girdle, and three guns upon his shoulder; and I took one pistol and the other three myself; and in this posture we marched out. I took a small bottle of rum in my pocket, and gave Friday a large bag with more powder and bullet. And as to orders, I charged him to keep close behind me, and not to stir, or shoot, or do anything till I bid him; and in the meantime not to speak a word. In this posture I fetched a compass to my right hand of near a mile, as well to get over the creek as to get into the wood; so that I might come within shot of them before I should be discovered, which I had seen by my glass it was easy to do.

While I was making this march, my former thoughts returning, I began to abate my resolution. I do not mean that I entertained any fear of their number; for as they were naked, unarmed wretches, it is certain I was superior to them — nay, though I had been alone; but it occurred to my thoughts, what call, what occasion, much less what necessity, I was in to go and dip my hands in blood, to attack people who had neither done nor intended me any wrong — who, as to me were innocent; and whose barbarous customs were their own disaster, being in them a token, indeed, of God's having left them, with the other nations of that part of the world to such stupidity and to such inhuman courses, but did not call me to take upon me to be a judge of their actions, much less an executioner of His justice: that whenever He thought fit, He would take the cause into His own hands, and by national vengeance punish them as a people for national crimes; but that, in the meantime, it was none of my business: but it was true Friday might justify it, because he was a declared enemy, and in a state of war with those very particular people, and it was lawful for him to attack them; but I could not say the same with respect to me. These things were so warmly pressed upon my thoughts, all the way as I went, that I resolved I would only go and place myself near them ,that I might observe their barbarous feast, and that I would act then as God should direct; but that unless some thing offered that was more a call to me than yet I knew of, I would not meddle with them.

With this reflection I entered the wood, and with all possible wariness and silence, Friday following close at my heels, I marched till I came to the skirt of the wood, on the side which was next to them. Here I called softly to Friday, and showing him a great tree, which was just at the corner of the wood, I bade him go to the tree and bring me word if he could see there plainly what they were doing. He did so, and came immediately back to me and told me they might be plainly viewed there; that they were all about their fire, eating the flesh of one of their prisoners; and that another lay bound upon the sand, a little from them, which he said they would kill next, and which fired all the very soul within me. He told me it was not one of their nation, but one of the bearded men who he had told me of, that came to their country in the boat. I was filled with horror at the very naming the white, bearded man, and going to the tree I saw plainly by my glass a white man who lay upon the beach of the sea, with his hands and his feet tied with flags, or things like rushes; and that he was a European, and had clothes on.

There was another tree, and a little thicket beyond it, about fifty yards nearer to them than the place where I was, which, by going a little way about, I saw I might come at undiscovered, and that then I should be within half-shot of them; so I withheld my passion, though I was, indeed, enraged to the highest degree, and going back about twenty paces, I got behind some bushes, which held all the way till I came to the other tree; and then I came to a little rising ground, which gave me a full view of them, at the distance of about eighty yards.

I had now not a moment to lose; for nineteen of the dreadful wretches sat upon the ground, all close huddled together, and had just sent the other two to butcher the poor Christian, and bring him perhaps limb by limb to their fire, and they were stooped down to untie the bands at his feet. I turned to Friday. "Now Friday," said I, "do as I bid thee." Friday said he would. "Then, Friday," said I, "do exactly as you see me do — fail in nothing." So I set down one of the muskets and the fowling-piece upon the ground, and Friday did the like by his; and with the other musket I took my aim at the savages, bidding him to do the like. Then asking him if he was ready, he said, "Yes." "Then fire at them," said I; and the same moment I fired also.

Friday took his aim so much better than I, that on the side that he shot he killed two of them, and wounded three more; and on my side, I killed one and wounded two. They were, you may be sure, in a dreadful consternation; and all of them who were not hurt jumped up upon their feet, but did not immediately know which way to run or which way to look — for they knew not from whence their destruction came. Friday kept his eyes close upon me, that, as I had bid him, he might observe what I did. So as soon as the first shot was made, I threw down the piece and took up the fowling-piece, and Friday did the like; he sees me cock and present; he did the same again. "Are you ready, Friday?" said I. "Yes," he says. "Let fly, then," said I, "in the name of God!" and with that I fired again among the amazed wretches, and so did Friday. And as our pieces were now loaded with what I called swan-shot, or small pistol bullets, we found only two drop; but so many were wounded, that they ran about yelling and screaming, like mad creatures, all bloody and miserably wounded, most of them; whereof three more fell quickly after, though not quite dead.

"Now, Friday," says I, laying down the discharged pieces, and taking up the musket which was yet loaded, "follow me," says I; which he did, with a great deal of courage. Upon which I rushed out of the wood and showed myself, and Friday close at my foot. As soon as I perceived they saw me, I shouted as loud as I could, and bade Friday do so too; and running as fast as I could, — which, by the way, was not very fast, being laden with arms as I was, — I made directly towards the poor victim, who was, as I said, lying upon the beach or shore, between the place where they sat and the sea. The two butchers, who were just going to work with him, had left him at the surprise of our first fire, and fled in a terrible fright to the seaside and had jumped into a canoe, and three more of the rest made the same way. I turned to Friday, and bid him step forward and fire at them. He understood me immediately, and running about forty yards to be near them, he shot at them, and I thought he had killed them all; for I saw them all fall of a heap into the boat; though I saw two of them up again quickly. However, he killed two of them, and wounded the third; so that he lay down in the bottom of the boat, as if he had been dead.

While my man Friday fired at them, I pulled out my knife and cut the flags that bound the poor victim, and loosing his hands and feet, I lifted him up, and asked him in the Portuguese tongue, "What he was?" He answered in Latin, "Christianus"; but was so weak and faint, that he could scarce stand or speak. I took my bottle out of my pocket and gave it him, making signs that he should drink, which he did; and I gave him a piece of bread, which he eat. Then I asked him, "What countryman he was?" And he said, "Espagniole"; and being a little recovered, let me know, by all the signs he could possibly make, how much he was in my debt for his deliverance. "Seignior," said I, with as much Spanish as I could make up, "we will talk afterwards, but we must fight now. If you have any strength left, take this pistol and sword and lay about you." He took them very thankfully; and no sooner had he the arms in his hands, but, as if they had put new vigour into him, he flew upon his murderers like a fury, and had cut two of them in pieces in an instant. For the truth is, as the whole was a surprise to them, so the poor creatures were so much frighted with the noise of our pieces, that they fell down for mere amazement and fear; and had no more power to attempt their own escape than their flesh had to resist our shot. And that was the case of those five that Friday shot at in the boat; for as three of them fell with the hurt they received, so the other two fell with the fright.

Those that were in the canoe worked hard to get out of gunshot; and though Friday made two or three shots at them, I did not find that he hit any of them. Friday would fain have had me take one of their canoes and pursue them; and indeed I was very anxious about their escape, lest, carrying the news home to their people, they should come back, perhaps, with two or three hundred of their canoes, and devour us by mere multitude. So I consented to pursue them by sea, and running to one of their canoes, I jumped in and bade Friday follow me; but when I was in the canoe I was surprised to find another poor creature lie there alive, bound hand and foot, as the Spaniard was, for the slaughter, and almost dead with fear, not knowing what the matter was; for he had not been able to look up over the side of the boat, he was tied so hard, neck and heels, and had been tied so long, that he had really but little life in him.

I immediately cut the twisted flags, or rushes, which they had bound him with, and would have helped him up; but he could not stand or speak, but groaned most piteously, believing, it seems still, that he was only unbound in order to be killed.

When Friday came to him, I bade him speak to him, and tell him of his deliverance, and pulling out my bottle, made him give the poor wretch a dram; which, with the news of his being delivered, revived him, and he sat up in the boat. But when Friday came to hear him speak, and look in his face, it would have moved anyone to tears to have seen how Friday kissed him, embraced him, hugged him, cried, laughed, hallooed, jumped about, danced, sung, then cried again, wrung his hands, beat his own face and head, and then sung and jumped about again like a distracted creature. It was a good while before I could make him speak to me, or tell me what was the matter; but when he came a little to himself, he told me that it was his father!

It is not easy for me to express how it moved me to see what ecstasy and filial affection had worked in this poor savage at the sight of his father and of his being delivered from death; nor indeed can I describe half the extravagances of his affection after this — for he went into the boat and out of the boat a great many times.

This action put an end to our pursuit of the canoe with the other savages, who were now gotten almost out of sight and it was happy for us that we did not; for it blew so hard within two hours after, and before they could be gotten a quarter of their way, and continued blowing so hard all night, and that from the north-west, which was against them, that I could not suppose their boat could live, or that they ever reached to their own coast.

But to return to Friday, he was so busy about his father that I could not find in my heart to take him off for some time. But after I thought he could leave him a little, I called him to me, and he came jumping and laughing and pleased to the highest extreme. Then I asked him if he had given his father any bread? He shook his head and said, "None. Ugly dog eat all up self." So I gave him a cake of bread out of a little pouch I carried on purpose; I also gave him a dram for himself, but he would not taste it, but carried it to his father.

I had in my pocket also two or three bunches of raisins, so I gave him a handful of them for his father. He had no sooner given his father these raisins but I saw him come out of the boat and run away as if he had been bewitched, he ran at such a rate — for he was the swiftest fellow of his foot that ever I saw; I say, he ran at such a rate that he was out of sight, as it were, in an instant; and though I called, and hallooed, too, after him it was all one, away he went, and in a quarter of an hour I saw him come back again, though not so fast as he went, and as he came nearer, I found his pace was slacker because he had something in his hand.

When he came up to me, I found he had been home for an earthen jug or pot to bring his father some fresh water, and that he had got two more cakes or loaves of bread. The bread he gave me, but the water he carried to his father. However, as I was very thirsty too, I took a little sup of it. This water revived his father more than all the rum or spirits I had given him; for he was just fainting with thirst.

When his father had drank, I called to him to know if there was any water left? He said, "Yes," and I bade him give it to the poor Spaniard, who was in as much want of it as his father; and I sent one of the cakes that Friday brought to the Spaniard too, who was indeed very weak, and was reposing himself upon a green place under the shade of a tree, and whose limbs were also very stiff and very much swollen with the rude bandage he had been tied with. When I saw that upon Friday's coming to him with the water, he sat up and drank, and took the bread and began to eat, I went to him and gave him a handful of raisins. He looked up in my face with all the tokens of gratitude and thankfulness that could appear in any countenance; but was so weak, notwithstanding he had so exterted himself in the fight, that he could not stand up upon his feet. He tried to do it two or tree times, but was really not able, his ankles were so swelled and so painful to him; so I bade him sit still, and caused Friday to rub his ankles and bathe them with rum.

I observed the poor affectionate creature every two minutes, or perhaps less, all the while he was here, turned his head about, to see if his father was in the same place and posture as he left him sitting; and at last he found he was not to be seen; at which he started up, and without speaking a word, flew with that swiftness to him, that one could scarce perceive his feet to touch the ground as he went. But when he came, he only found he had laid himself down to ease his limbs; so Friday came back to me presently, and then I spoke to the Spaniard to let Friday help him up if he could, and lead him to the boat, and then he should carry him to our dwelling where I would take care of him. But Friday, a lusty strong fellow, took the Spaniard quite up upon his back, and carried him away to the boat, and set him down softly upon the side or gunwale of the canoe, with his feet in the inside of it and then lifted him quite in, and set him close to his father, and presently stepping out again, launched the boat off, and paddled it along the shore faster than I could walk, though the wind blew pretty hard too. So he brought them both safe to our creek; and leaving them in the boat, runs away to fetch the other canoe. And as he passed me I spoke to him, and asked him whither he went? He told me, "Go fetch more boat." So away he went like the wind, for sure never man or horse run like him; and he had the other canoe in the creek almost as soon as I got to it by land.

My island was now peopled, and I thought myself very rich in subjects. And it was a merry reflection which I frequently made, how like a king I looked. First of all the whole country was my own mere property; so that I had an undoubted right of dominion. Secondly, my people were perfectly subjected; I was absolute lord and lawgiver; they all owed their lives to me, and were ready to lay down their lives, if there had been occasion of it, for me.

I then began to enter into a little conversation with my two new subjects. And first I set Friday to enquire of his father what he thought of the escape of the savages in that canoe, and whether we might expect a return of them with a power too great for us to resist. His first opinion was, that the savages in the boat never could live out the storm which blew that night they went off, but must of necessity be drowned or driven south to those other shores where they were as sure to be devoured as they were to be drowned if they were cast away. But as to what they would do if they came safe on shore, he said he knew not; but it was his opinion that they were so dreadfully frighted with the manner of their being attacked — the noise and the fire — that he believed they would tell their people they were all killed by thunder and lightning, not by the hand of man; and that the two which appeared — namely, Friday and me — were two heavenly spirits of furies come down to destroy them, and not men with weapons.

I had a serious discourse with the Spaniard, and when I understood that there were sixteen more of his countrymen and Portuguese, who, having been cast away and made their escape to that side, lived there at peace indeed with the savages, but were very sore put to it for necessaries, and indeed for life. I asked him all the particulars of their voyage, and found they were a Spanish ship bound from the Rio de la Plata to the Havannah, being directed to leave their loading there, which was chiefly hides and silver, and to bring back what European goods they could meet with there; that they had five Portuguese seamen on board, who they took out of another wreck; that five of their own men were drowned when the first ship was lost, and that these escaped through infinite dangers and hazards, and arrived almost starved on the Cannibal coast, where they expected to have been devoured every moment.

I asked him how he thought they would receive a proposal from me which might tend towards an escape? and whether, if they were all here, it might not be done? I told him with freedom I feared mostly their treachery and ill-usage of me if I put my life in their hands.

He answered, with a great deal of candour and ingenuity, that their condition was so miserable, and they were so sensible of it that he believed they would abhor the thought of using any man unkindly that should contribute to their deliverance; and that if I pleased, he would go to them with the old man, and discourse with them about it, and return again, and bring me their answer: that he would make conditions with them upon their solemn oath, that they should be absolutely under my leading as their comander and captain. He would bring a contract from them under their hands for that purpose.

Then he told me he would first swear to me himself, that he would never stir from me as long as he lived till I gave him orders; and that he would take my side to the last drop of his blood if there should happen the least breach of faith among his countrymen.

He told me they were all of them very civil, honest men, and they were under the greatest distress imaginable, having neither weapons nor clothes nor any food, but at the mercy and discretion of the savages; out of all hopes of ever returning to their own country; and that he was sure, if I would undertake their relief, they would live and die by me.

Upon these assurances, I resolved to venture to relieve them if possible, and to send the old savage and the Spaniard over to them to treat; but when we had gotten all things in a readiness to go, the Spaniard himself started an objection.

He told me he thought it would be more advisable to let him and the two other dig and cultivate some more land, as much as I could spare seed to sow; and that we should wait another harvest, that we might have as supply of corn for his countrymen when they should come; for want might be a temptation to them to disagree, or not think themselves delivered otherwise than out of one difficulty into another.

CHAPTER SEVENTEEN

It was now harvest, and our crop in good order. It was not the most plentiful increase I had seen in the island, but, however, it was enough to answer our end; for from our twenty-two bushels of barley we brought in and thrashed out above two hundred and twenty bushels, and the like in proportion of the rice; which was store enough for our food to the next harvest, though all the sixteen Spaniards had been on shore with me; or if we had been ready for a voyage, it would very plentifully have victualled our ship.

When we had thus housed and secured our magazine of corn, we fell to work to make more wickerwork, namely, great baskets in which we kept it; and the Spaniard was very handy and dexterous at this part, and often blamed me that I did not make some things for defence of this kind of work; but I saw no need of it.

And now having a full supply of food for all the guests I expected, I gave the Spaniard leave to go over to the main to see what he could do with those he had left behind him there.

Under these instructions, the Spaniard and the old savage, the father of Friday, went away in one of the canoes. I gave each of them a musket and a firelock on it, and about eight charges of powder and ball, charging them to be very good husbands of both, and not use either of them but upon urgent occasion.

It was no less than eight days I waited for them, when a strange and unforeseen accident intervened. I was fast asleep in my hutch one morning, when my man Friday came running in to me and called aloud, "Master, master, they are come, they are come!"

I jumped up, and regardless of danger, I went without my arms, which was not my custom to do; but I was surprised, when, turning my eyes to the set, I presently saw a boat at about a league and a half's distance, standing in for the shore with a shoulder-of-mutton sail, as they call it; and the wind blowing pretty fair to bring them in. Upon this I called Friday in, and bid him lie close, for these were not the people we looked for, and that we might not know yet whether they were friends or enemies.

In the next place, I went in to fetch my perspective-glass to see what I could make of them; and having taken the ladder out, I climbed up to the top of the hill.

I had scarce set my foot on the hill, when my eye plainly discovered a ship lying at an anchor, at about two leagues and a half's distance from me south-south-east, but not above a league and a half from the shore. By my observation it appeared plainly to be an English ship, and the boat appeared to be an English long-boat.

I had not kept myself long in this posture, but I saw the boat draw near the shore, as if they looked for a creek to thrust in at for the convenience of landing. However, as they did not come quite far enough, they did not see the little inlet where I formerly landed my rafts, but run their boat on shore upon the beach, at about half a mile from me.

When they were on shore, I was fully satisfied that they were Englishmen, at least most of them. They were in all eleven men, whereof three of them I found were unarmed, and, as I thought, bound; and when the first four or five of them were jumped on shore, they took these three out of the boat as prisoners.

I had no thought of what the matter really was, but stood trembling with the horror of the sight, expecting every moment when the three prisoners should be killed; nay, once I saw one of the villains lift up his arm with a great cutlass, as the seamen call it, or sword, to strike one of the poor men.

After I had observed the outrageous usage of the three men by the insolent seamen, I observed the fellows run scattering about the land, as if they wanted to see the country. I observed that the three other men had liberty to go also where they pleased; but they sat down all three upon the ground, very pensive, and looked like men in despair.

Upon this I resolved to discover myself to them, and learn something of their condition. I came as near them undiscovered as I could, and then, before any of them saw me, I called aloud to them in Spanish, "What are ye, gentlemen?"

They started up at the noise, but were ten times more confounded when they saw me, and the uncouth figure that I made. They made no answer at all, but I thought I perceived them just going to fly from me, when I spoke to them in English. "Gentlemen," said I, "do not be surprised at me; perhaps you may have a friend near you when you did not expect it."

"Our case," said one, "sir, is too long to tell you while our murderers are so near; but, in short, sir, I was commander of that ship; my men have mutinied against me; they have been hardly prevailed on not to murder me, and in last have set me on shore in this desolate place, with these two men with me; one my mate, the other a passenger."

"Look you, sir," said I, "if I venture your deliverance, are you willing to make two conditions with me?" He anticipated my proposals by telling me that both he and the ship, if recovered, should be wholly directed and commanded by me in everything.

"Well," says I, "my conditions are but two. 1. That while you stay on this island with me you will not pretend to any authority here. 2. That if the ship is, or may be recovered, you will carry me and my man to England passage free."

He gave me all the assurances that the invention and faith of man could devise, that he would comply with these most reasonable demands, and besides would owe his life to me, and he acknowledged it upon all occasion as long as he lived.

"Well, then," said I, "here are three muskets for you, with powder and ball; tell me next what you think is proper to be done."

He said very modestly, that he was loath to kill them if he could help it, but that two were incorrigible villains, and had been the authors of all the mutiny in the ship, and if they escaped we should be undone still; for they would go on board and bring the whole ship's company, and destroy us all.

Animated, he took the musket I had given him in his hand, and a pistol in his belt, and his two comrades with him, with each man a piece in his hand. The two men who were with him, going first made some noise, at which one of the seamen who was awake turned about, and seeing them coming, cried out to the rest. But it was too late then; for the moment he cried out they fired. They had so well aimed their shot at the men they knew, that one of them was killed on the spot, and the other very much wounded; but not being dead, he started up upon his feet, and called eagerly for help to the other; but the captain, stepping to him, told him it was too late to cry for help, he should call upon God to forgive his villainy, and with that word knocked him down with the stock of his musket, so that he never spoke more. They were three more in the company, and one of them was also slightly wounded. By this time I was come, and when they saw their danger, and that it was in vain to resist, they begged for mercy. The captain told them he would spare their lives, which I was not against; only I obliged him to keep them bound hand and foot while they were upon the island.

While this was doing, I sent Friday with the captain's mate to the boat, with orders to secure her and bring away the oars and sail; which they did. And by and by, three straggling men, that were (happily for them) parted from the rest, came back upon hearing the guns fired; and seeing their captain, who before was their prisoner, they submitted to be bound also, and so our victory was complete.

It now remained that the captain and I should consider how to recover the ship. He told me he was perfectly at a loss what measures to take; for that there were still six-and-twenty hands on board, who, having entered into a cursed conspiracy, by which they had all forfeited their lives to the law, would be hardened in it now by desperation.

Upon this it presently occurred to me that in a little while the ship's crew, wondering what was become of their comrades and of the boat, would certainly come on shore in their other boat to see for them. I told him the first thing we had to do was to stave that boat which lay upon the beach, so that they might not carry her off; and taking everything out of her, leave her so far useless as not to be fit to swim. Accordingly, we went on board, took the arms which were left on board out of her, and whatever else we found there, then we knocked a great hole in her bottom, that if they had come strong enough to master us, yet they could not carry off the boat.

While we heaved the boat up upon the beach, so high that the tide would not float her off a high-water mark; and besides, had broke a hole in her bottom too big to be quickly stopped, we heard the ship fire a gun.

At last, when all their signals and firings proved fruitless, and they found the boat did not stir, we saw them, by the help of my glasses, hoist another boat out, and row towards the shore; and we found as they approached that there was no less than ten men in her, and that they had firearms with them.

Seven men came on shore and the three who remained in the boat put her off to a good distance from the shore, and came to an anchor to wait for them, so that it was impossible for us to come at them in the boat.

Those that came on shore kept close together, marching towards the top of the little hill under which my habitation lay; and we could see them plainly, though they could not perceive us.

We waited a great while, though very impatient for their removing; and were very uneasy when, after long consultations, we saw them start all up and march down towards the sea.

As soon as I perceived them go towards the shore, I ordered Friday and the captain's mate to go over the little creek westward, towards the place where the savages came on shore when Friday was rescued; and as soon as they came to a little rising ground, at about half a mile distance, I bade them halloo as loud as they could, and wait till they found the seamen heard them; that as soon as ever they heard the seamen answer them they should return it again; and then, keeping out of sight, take a round, always answering when the other hallooed, to draw them as far into the island, and among the woods, as possible, and then wheel about again to me by such ways as I directed them.

They were just going into the boat when Friday and the mate hallooed; and they presently heard them, and answering, run along the shore westward, towards the voice they heard, when they were presently stopped by the creek, where the water being up, they could not get over, and called for the boat to come up and set them over, as indeed I expected.

When they had set themselves over, I observed that the boat, being gone up a good way into the creek, and, as it were, in a harbour within the land, they took one of the three men out of her to go along with them, and left only two in the boat, having fastened her to the stump of a little tree on the shore.

This was what I wished for, and immediately leaving Friday and the captain's mate to their business, I took the rest with me, and crossing the creek out of their sight, we surprised the two men before they were aware; one of them lying on shore, and the other being in the boat. The fellow on shore was between sleeping and waking, and going to start up, the captain, who was foremost, ran in upon him, and knocked him down, and then called out to him in the boat to yield, or he was a dead man.

There needed very few arguments to persuade a single man to yield when he saw five men upon him, and his comrade knocked down; besides, this was, it seems, one of the three who were not so hearty in the mutiny as the rest of the crew, and therefore, was easily persuaded not only to yield, but afterwards to join very sincerely with us.

In the meantime, Friday and the captain's mate so well managed their business with the rest, that they drew them, by hallooing and answering, from one hill to another, and from one wood to another, till they not only heartily tired them, but left them where they were very sure they could not reach back to the boat before it was dark; and indeed they were heartily tired themselves also by the time they came back to us.

We had nothing now to do but to watch for them in the dark, and to fall upon them, so as to make sure work with them.

It was several hours after Friday came back to me before they came back to their boat; and we could hear the foremost of them long before they came quite up, calling to those behind to come along; and could also hear them answer and complain how lame and tired they were, and not able to come any faster — which was very welcome news to us.

At length they came up to the boat; but 'tis impossible to express their confusion when they found the boat fast aground in the creek, the tide ebbed out, and their two men gone!

My men would fain have me give them leave to fall upon them at once in the dark; but I was willing to take them at some advantage so to spare them, and kill as few of them as I could; and especially I was unwilling to hazard the killing any of our own men, knowing the other were very well armed. But when they came nearer, the captain and Friday starting up on their feet, let fly at them.

The boatswain was killed upon the spot, the next man was shot into body, and fell just by him, and the third run for it.

At the noise of the fire I immediately advanced with my whole army, which was now eight men, namely, myself generalissimo, Friday my lieutenant-general, the captain and his two men, and the three prisoners of war, who we had trusted with arms.

So taken by surprise were they that they all laid down their arms, and begged their lives; and then my great army of eight men, came up and seized upon them all, and upon their boat — only that I kept myself and one more out of sight, for reasons of state.

Our next work was to repair the boat, and think of seizing the ship; and as for the captain, now he had leisure to parley with them, he expostulated with them upon the villainy of their practices with him, and at length upon the farther wickedness of their design, and how certainly it must bring them to misery and distress in the end, and perhaps to the gallows.

I asked the captain if he was willing to venture on board the ship; for as for me and my man Friday, I did not think it was proper for us to stir, having seven men left behind, and it was employment enough for us to keep them asunder and supply them with their victuals.

The captain had no difficulty before him but to furnish his two boats, stop the breach of one, and man them. He made his passenger captain of one, with four other men; and himself, and his mate and five men, went in the other. And they continued to contrive their business very well, for they came up to the ship about midnight, and the ship was taken effectually, with few lives lost.

CHAPTER EIGHTEEN

As soon as the ship was thus secured, the captain ordered seven guns to be fired, which was the signal agreed upon with me to give me notice of his succes; which, you may be sure, I was very glad to hear, having sat watching upon the shore for it till near two of the clock in the morning.

Having thus heard the signal plainly, I laid me down; and it having been a day of great fatigue to me, I slept very sound till I was something surprised with the noise of a gun; and presently starting up, I heard a man call me by the name of "Governor, governor;" and presently I knew the captain's voice, when climbing up to the top of the hill, there he stood, and pointing to the ship he embraced me in his arms. "My dear friend and deliverer," says he, "there's your ship; for she is all yours, and so are we and all that belong to her."

It was a very kind and agreeable present, as any one may imagine, to one in my circumstances. After these ceremonies past, we began to consult what was to be done with the prisoners we had; for it was worth considering whether we might venture to take them away with us or no, especially two of them, who we knew to be incorrigible and refractory to the last degree; and the captain said, he knew they were such rogues that there was no obliging them, and if he did carry them away it must be in irons as malefactors to be delivered over to justice at the first English colony he could come at. And I found that the captain himself was very anxious about it.

Upon this, I told him that if he desired I durst undertake to bring the man to make it their own request that he should leave them upon the island. "I should be very glad of that," says the captain, "with all my heart."

"Well," says I, "I will send for them up, and talk with them for you." So I caused Friday and the two hostages — for they were now discharged, their comrades having performed their promise; I say, I caused them to bring up the five men, pinioned, to the bower, and keep them there till I came.

Being all met, and the captain with me, I caused the men to be brought before me; and I told them I had had a full account of their villainous behaviour to the captain, and how they had run away with the ship, and were prepared to commit farther robberies.

I let them know that by my direction the ship had been seized, that she lay now in the road; and they might see by and by that their new captain had received the reward of his villainy, for that they might see him hanging at the yard-arm.

One of them answered in the name of the rest, that they had nothing to say to this, but that when they were taken the captain promised them their lives; and they humbly implored my mercy. But I told them I knew not what mercy to show them; for as for myself I had resolved to quit the island with all my men, and had taken passage with the captain to go for England. However, if they desired that I had some inclination to give them their lives, if they thought they could shift on shore.

They seemed very thankful for it, said they would much rather venture to stay there than to be carried to England to be hanged.

When they had all declared their willingness to stay, I then told them I would let them into the story of my living there, and put them into the way of making it easy to them. Accordingly, I gave them the whole history of the place and of my coming to it; showed them my fortifications, the way I made my bread, planted my corn, cured my grapes; and in a word, all that was necessary to make them easy. I told them the story also of the sixteen Spaniards that were to be expected; for whom I left a letter, and made them promise to treat them in common with themselves.

I left them my firearms, namely, five muskets, three fowling-pieces, and three swords. I had above a barrel and a half of powder left; for after the first year or two I used but little and wasted none. I gave them a description of the way I managed the goats and directions to milk and fatten them, and to make both butter and cheese.

In a word, I gave them every part of my own story. And I told them I would prevail with the captain to leave them two barrels of gunpowder more, and some garden-seeds, which I told them I would have been very glad of; also I gave them the bag of peas which the captain had brought me to eat, and bade them be sure to sow and increase them.

Having done all this, I left them the next day and went on board the ship. We prepared immediately to sail.

When I took leave of this island I carried on board for relics the great goat-skin cap I had made, my umbrella, and my parrot; also I forgot not to take the money I formerly mentioned, which had lain by me so long useless that it was grown rusty, or tarnished, and could hardly pass for silver till it had been a little rubbed and handled; as also the money I found in the wreck of the Spanish ship.

And thus I left the island the 19th of December, as I found by the ship's account, in the year 1686, after I had been upon it eight and twenty years, two months, and nineteen days.

THE END

OTHER TITLES IN THIS SERIES

Published by Peter Haddock Ltd.,
Bridlington, England.©
Printed in India.